MW01103718

Advance Praise for *Agenda*:

"*Leave it to Wood to tackle today's societal issues in a great cozy mystery! Loved it!*

—Marilyn C.

"*There isn't one Colbie Colleen book I haven't read because they're all wonderful—and, Agenda is just as good! Wood's characters are so vivid, it's easy to relate. A great read!*"

—J. Winfield

"*I've been a Colbie Colleen fan since Wood's first book—and, after reading her latest book, I still am! A fun read!*"

—Bethany Williams

"*After reading every one of Wood's books in the Colbie Colleen series, I can honestly say I'd rather read hers instead of some of the mystery greats. Always refreshing, the story flies by, and I find myself hoping for more—Agenda is no exception!*"

— Tony Lidell

"*Such a fun, cozy mystery read!*"

—L.R. Simmons

"*Agenda is like every other Colbie Colleen book—impossible to put down!*"

—Meaghan Stills

AGENDA

AGENDA

Faith Wood

Wood Media
British Columbia, Canada

Copyright © 2021 Faith Wood
Agenda
First Edition, Paperback 2021

All rights reserved. You may not use or reproduce by any means including graphic, electronic, or mechanical, photocopying, recording, taping, or by any information storage retrieval system without the written permission of the publisher. The only exception is using brief quotations embodied in critical articles or reviews.

ISBN: 978-1-63760-070-2

Printed in the United States of America

DEDICATION

To all Colbie Colleen fans . . .

In 2015—when I began writing my first, award-winning cozy, suspense mystery novel, *the Accidental Audience*—never did I imagine I'd go on to write seven more! But, I did, today writing the final words of my eighth manuscript!

It's been such a gratifying experience, so I want you to be the first to know—in late spring of this year, I'll be introducing my new series, Book 1 entitled, *Where Truth Goes to Die, a Decklin Kilgarry Cozy Suspense Mystery*, and I'm eager to introduce him to you!

So, I thank you for your kind words and faithful following of Colbie Colleen—you are my inspiration!

CHAPTER 1

The best thing after a long day in the courtroom? A hot shower, jammies, and a cup of hot chocolate. For Colbie, it was the perfect end to a day of witness testimony, her eagerly anticipated words carrying weight for the defense. As much as she disliked the disruption in her life, it was her duty to speak the truth—and, if the prosecution didn't like what she had to say?

Well—that was the point, wasn't it?

By the end of her time on the stand, energy sizzled in the gallery, most realizing there was no way in hell Garrison McNamara was guilty of second-degree murder. Despite what other witnesses claimed—few carrying credible credentials—both camps were leaning toward believing Colbie.

To do otherwise would be foolish.

Thank God that's over, she thought as she placed the steaming cup of chocolate on the end table by the couch. Propping her feet up on the ottoman, she melted into the soft leather, enjoying how its soft cushions cradled her back. Ever since her recent case in Georgia, it hadn't been the same, lightning-strike pain rendering her nearly immobile when at its worst. In fact, it was only by the grace of God she could continue working, some days worse than others. *Still,* she thought, *maybe I should have it checked . . .*

Within ten, a dreamless sleep—until she heard her name. "Colbie . . ."

Twitching slightly, she shifted her position.

"Colbie . . ."

As if she didn't want to but had no choice, she slowly opened her eyes, unsure of what she heard. "Colbie—it's me. Daria . . ."

Of course, it wasn't every day Colbie's best friend came to her as an apparition, and the fact she appeared as Colbie slept?

Colbie knew it wasn't good.

She watched as her friend stood by the ottoman, face ashen and unclear, her eyes hollow orbs—and, it was in that moment and with a flash of clarity, Colbie knew.

Her friend was dead.

Stunned, she watched as Daria gestured to her using sign language—it made perfect sense, too, since she was a tenured teacher with a renowned international sign language institute. Her fingers flew as she tried to communicate, urgency apparent—the only problem was Colbie had no idea what she was saying.

Moments later, Daria waved a tender goodbye, the apparition fading to an eventual wisp—then, nothing. Colbie's eyes welled as she thought of the possibilities, none making sense as she glanced at the clock on the wall.

Shortly past midnight.

Promising to call Daria's mom first thing in the morning, Colbie laid on the couch, tears streaming. Finally, she drifted off, her heart heavy.

Her mind numb.

CHAPTER 2

There was no mistaking the senator's displeasure as he sputtered a little too close to his assistant's face. "I don't give a crap what you have to do—get Derrick Dickson in here within the hour!"

The assistant stepped back, most likely to fend off flying spittle, her face flushed with budding anger. "I'll try, Sir . . ."

"You'll do more than try, Constance! If he's not standing in my office at two, don't bother coming to work tomorrow!"

"You'll fire me?"

More errant spittle. "That's not all! I guarantee you won't work in Washington again . . ."

"I'll do my best . . ." With that, Constance Parnell was out the door, hoping she could get away fast enough before he thought of something else. Although in his employ for over two decades, it was the first time she considered covering her own ass while working for Harold Stanton, Virginia's longest standing senator.

Abrasive from the first time he hit the senate floor, after three decades of accomplishing absolutely nothing, it was no secret colleagues on the other side regarded him as incorrigible and slightly off his rocker. Most figured he was no longer relevant, yet his clout extended far beyond hallowed walls. But, the truth?

Most hated Harold Stanton's guts.

Some swore he was as sharp as he was thirty years prior, yet others knew—Harry was walking within the shadows of age and, as with most D.C. politicians, hopefuls waited in the wings to snatch his position at just the right time. Yet, the old curmudgeon refused to budge—retirement simply didn't appeal.

Money and status did.

Somehow, the planets miraculously aligned, Derrick Dickson knocking on Stanton's door precisely at two. "Another crisis, Harry?" He shut it softly behind him, then took a seat in front of the senator's desk.

Stanton shot him a look, advising he was in no mood for inconsequential smalltalk. "We have things to discuss."

"Things?"

Stanton focused on the man sitting across from him, instantly repulsed by everything his colleague deemed important. "Something's coming . . ."

"That's dramatic . . ." A smirk tugged at Dickson's lips, knowing it would infuriate his colleague.

"And, dramatic it will be if what I think is going to happen actually transpires . . ."

"Which is?"

"Our country will be tested like never before . . ."

Dickson sighed, then stood. "You're talking in riddles, Harry—and, you're wasting my time." A ballsy move, even for a seasoned senator—but, Derrick knew, as did everyone who had to deal with Harry Stanton, the day was coming when the Virginia senator could no longer hide his mind didn't work like it used to. When that day arrived?

Derrick Dickson was waiting in the wings.

There was little doubt the country was ripe for sweeping change—and, if he had his way? He'd be there to step in— you know, pick up the pieces. It was something he dreamed of since the time he was in high school, thinking about the day he would become a touted name on the beltway, everyone knowing who he was—just not the core of who he was becoming. "If you have something to discuss, Harry, put it in writing . . ." He headed for the door, knowing Stanton was probably sopping up spit from attempting to utter falsely righteous indignation.

Stanton watched him leave, disgust rising in his throat. *How dare you*, he thought, his eyes on Dickson until he disappeared from view. Again, he recalled the situation at hand—to do nothing would be foolish.

To announce his concerns would be his demise.

"I can't believe it," Colbie sobbed, sorrow impaling her soul. "What happened?"

Janelle Bendix said nothing for a moment, her pain as excruciating as her daughter's friend's. "It was so quick—and, Daria thought it was nothing more than a cold!"

"She took ill?"

"Yes—we finally insisted on taking her to emergency, and . . ."

Colbie waited patiently, knowing their conversation was probably one of the worst either of them would have. Finally, a gentle prompt. "What happened, Janelle?"

"Three days later she was dead . . ." With more anguish than she could possibly endure, Janelle's heart fractured one more time.

Fifteen minutes later, Colbie clicked off, emotions shredded—until the hair on her arms suddenly raised as if being coached by an inexplicable, low-grade electricity.

Closing her eyes, she waited only a few seconds until the scent of her friend was directly in front of her. After the first time Daria appeared, Colbie knew what to expect, knowing she was about to receive another message.

Again, Daria Bendix's fingers flew, spelling out whatever it was she wanted Colbie to know and, again, Colbie couldn't understand.

"What are you telling me, Daria? I don't get it . . ."

Suddenly, her friend began to dissipate as if she no longer had the energy to continue the conversation. Within seconds, she was gone, leaving Colbie broken and alone, wondering what Daria was trying to say. Then, resolve strengthening its grip, she sat up a little straighter and swiped at her tears with the back of her hand, making a promise to herself and to the woman who always had her back. *I'll figure out what you're trying to tell me, if it's the last thing I do . . .*

With silent proclamation, Colbie grabbed her laptop from the coffee table, trying to recall the name of the sign language institute where Daria taught. Within seconds, her search began—whatever it was her friend needed her to know had to be important.

If not critical.

Derrick Dickson didn't notice office lights flicking off as his colleagues decided a twelve-hour day was enough. The conversation with Harry Stanton still fresh in his mind, there was something about it making Dickson's skin crawl. There was little doubt the old man wasn't the sharpest knife in the drawer, but, for some bizarre reason?

There was a chance Harry Stanton was right.

Although he didn't mention it, he, too, felt a shift. *Maybe it's the weather,* he thought, glancing at rain pelting the window. The city's sultry, humid summer was causing tempers to flare, not only on the streets of metropolitan and urban areas, but within the walls of Congress, as well. *It's as if someone flipped a switch . . .* Twenty-plus years on the hill provided his own brand of experience—and, that evening?

It was telling him to watch his back.

With uncomfortable realization, he supposed it might not have been the smartest move when he left Stanton's office before hearing what he had to say. Still, knowing there'd been more fiction than truth in Harry's stories over the last few years, one couldn't help but wonder.

"You done for the night?" Jake Powers grinned, inviting himself in, taking a seat in front of Dickson's desk. "You look like you were deep in thought . . ."

"I was . . ." Derrick hesitated, knowing if he brought up Harry Stanton there could be blowback down the road— for what reason, he didn't know. "Have you talked to Harry lately," he finally asked, leaning back in his chair.

"Stanton? No, not really—I don't see much of him since we're on different committees." The seasoned Washington State senator's smiled faded, noticing his colleague had something important on his mind. "Why? What's going on with Stanton?"

"I'm not sure—but, when I left him earlier today, I had a weird feeling . . ."

"Who doesn't after being with Harry for five minutes?"

"You're right about that," Dickson smiled, "but, this was different. He kind of reminded me of Burt Lancaster in *Elmer Gantry* . . ."

Jake said nothing, trying to place the reference. "Sorry, man—I'm not a movie guy."

"Burt Lancaster played the role of Elmer Gantry, who was a tent preacher, but really a fast-talking con man."

"What does that have to do with Harry?"

Dickson shook his head. "Damned if I know—but, it's like he's trying to convince me of something and, in my gut, I don't want any part of it."

"That's it?"

"I was only with him for a few minutes before he started talking of some sort of coming change . . ."

"Seriously?"

A nod. "He said it'll be of such magnitude, it will change our country . . ."

Senator Powers was quiet, thinking of his last run-in with Harry Stanton. "Man, that's just Harry—he's been spouting stuff like that for years! You know that . . ."

And, that was the thing. Derrick did know it—that time, however?

There was something about Harry . . .

Within the week, Colbie flew to Ohio for Daria's funeral service, the church packed with those who knew her best. Always a beacon of light in anyone's life, to Colbie, her friend's passing was incomprehensible.

Amidst tears and laughter, friends recalled their treasured times with the woman who couldn't wait to immerse herself in sign language. Initially, her thought was to work at the U.N. as an interpreter—but, the second she had the opportunity to work with people who struggled in their every day lives because of hearing loss?

They stole her heart.

Rounding the corner to a new decade, by the time Daria turned thirty, she was working abroad, inspiring and motivating educators throughout Europe. As she and Colbie slipped into middle age with barely noticing, there wasn't a soul in the education biz who didn't know her name. Somehow, she managed to bridge barriers, bringing life to those who couldn't hear.

For Colbie? Daria Bendix was her sounding board, and she could talk to her about anything without fear of sounding like a complete idiot. "Those are the friends we have for life," she told Janelle as they offered tearful goodbyes. "In this one, and the next . . ."

Janelle said nothing as she watched Colbie climb into her cab, then pull from the curb knowing she may never see her daughter's friend again. Life would go on—full for some, a little less for others. And, as days would undoubtedly pass, there would be less laughter for both to enjoy.

So, as Colbie's car pulled from sight, both felt a scorching sorrow . . .

One changing them for all time.

"Have you talked to her since she got back from her gig in Georgia?" Kevin didn't look at his partner as he asked the question—he thought he knew the answer, but figured it was always wise to confirm.

"Only for a few minutes—and, it wasn't a good time to talk."

"Why?"

Ryan was quiet, thinking of the woman for whom he'd give his life if she asked. "Her best friend died . . ."

"Seriously?" Kevin sat in front of Ryan's desk, cracked open his bottled water then took a gulp. "How was she? Colbie, I mean . . ."

"Not good—she mentioned she was going to find out what happened, though."

"Suspicious circumstances?"

"Who knows? But, if Colbie is going to investigate something, there's probably something to it . . ."

"Did she ask for our help?"

Ryan shook his head. "Nope—but, like I said, we only talked for a minute or two. It wasn't a good time . . ."

Both men knew such an abbreviated conversation with Colbie was unusual even in the worst of circumstances. Since she decided to back out of their investigation business, she always made it a point to keep in touch every so often, conversations, of course, including her possible return. Even so, nothing was definitive, and Colbie shrank from making a decision.

"Did she say she'd get in touch," Kevin asked, silently hoping the woman who plucked him out of Savanna, Georgia, offering a life more exciting than he could imagine, would return to the business.

"Within the week . . ."

"Think she will?"

"I have no idea . . ."

CHAPTER 3

*H*arry Stanton looked at himself in the mirror, the bathroom light subtle and accommodating. *For an old geezer,* he thought as he rubbed the stubble on his face with both palms, *you don't look too bad!*

As his wife stirred in bed, he softly closed the door—a light sleeper, she never did get used to her husband's early hours. A night owl by her own admission, morning truly didn't start until the sun had been up for the better part of the morning. In their early married life, it was cause for contention, but, as years passed and they mellowed into each other, neither really cared, anymore.

Within thirty, Harry was out the door, knowing he'd be first in line at his favorite coffee shop. Washington came alive early, commuters often opting for the before-dawn trains, hoping to beat those vying for a coveted spot. Routines became essential, and it was Harry's to spend the first hours of his day catching up on the overnight news with a cup of coffee. That day?

A headline that couldn't possibly be true.

Derrik Dickson adjusted his tie, then grabbed his shoes and sat on end of the bed. Using the petrified wood shoe horn his father gave him for his fortieth birthday, he slipped into his right shoe, listening as an anchor on an early morning news show laid down stories of the day, one in particular catching his attention. "If the allegations are true," the young woman reported, "it will certainly be of critical national importance . . ."

"What will be of critical importance," his wife asked from the bed, opening one eye.

Left shoe. "I don't know—I didn't catch the first part." But, whatever it was, there was a feeling in his gut he didn't like—one he didn't have only moments before. "Don't count on me for dinner," he commented as he grabbed his suit coat, then planted a quick peck on her cheek. "It's going to be a late night . . ."

With that he was out the door, the young reporter's words heavy on his mind. *Is that what Stanton was talking about*, he wondered as he unlocked the car. Still considering his unanswered question, his next thought caused a change in his day's events. First up?

A chat with Harry Stanton.

"Colbie? Colbie Colleen?" Jake Powers gave her a quick hug accompanied by a kid-like grin. "Last I heard, I think you were . . . well, I don't remember where you were, but I know it wasn't here!" He looked at her, appreciating how great she looked in running gear.

Colbie laughed, enjoying the few moments of attention. "You're right—I was gone, but now I'm back!" She looked up at him, recalling what it was like when they dated when she was a junior in high school in her hometown. For a while, everyone talked about them until Jake moved to the city, leaving her to pick up the pieces of their budding relationship. "Is Congress on break?"

Nodding, he gestured to the street bench. "Yep—but, I have a feeling we're going to be called back." He turned slightly so he could see her better. "You look great!" He paused, thinking. "How long has it been?"

"To many to count!" She smiled, thinking of their time together so many years ago.

"Geez! I can't believe it . . ."

So, there they sat for the better part of an hour, neither paying attention to passersby as they caught up on years of life. Married twenty years prior, Jake and his wife were parents of twin girls entering high school within the coming weeks—it was when his wife was expecting he made the decision to jump into politics. "I just didn't like the way things were going," he commented. "But, that's a story for another time—should we get together for lunch before I head back to D.C.? Susie would love to meet you!"

Colbie couldn't help laughing. "Your wife is interested in meeting your old girlfriend? Somehow, I doubt that . . ."

"It's true! When you cracked the case of your boyfriend's kidnapping? I told her I knew you . . ."

"Well, I don't know—let's play it by ear. If you have time, get it touch . . ."

Without hesitation, Jake grabbed his cell. "Number?"

"I'm afraid I was rude to you, Harry—and, I apologize." Derrick Dickson extended his hand. "When you tried to talk to me a few days ago, I was having a bad day—although, I'm the first to admit that isn't an excuse." A pause. "I hope we can move forward . . ."

Stanton accepted the handshake, then invited his colleague to join him for a before-lunch cocktail. "It will take the edge off, my friend . . ."

"Thank you . . ." An insincere appreciation, the thought of drinking before noon was repugnant to Dickson, but what harm could it do? Besides, there was nothing like a touch of alcohol to get tongues wagging, and Derrick certainly wanted to know what Stanton had to say.

It was good timing, too—most senators were on break with only a few deciding to stay in the city. Stanton and Derrick were of the mind they could get more done without constant interruptions—not that they ever had privacy, but there was less chance of prying ears and eyes.

"When we last met," Dickson began, "you hinted at something I couldn't get out of my mind . . ."

Stanton turned, ice cube tongs in hand. "Hinted? You didn't seem too eager to hear about it then, Derrick—what changed your mind?"

"Again, Harry, I apologize—I was being a complete ass." A pause. "But, to answer your question, when I considered it was coming from you, whatever it is you wanted to tell me will be from a trusted source . . ."

A line of bullshit? Of course! After all, Derrick Dickson was a highly regarded politician—B.S. was a part of who he was, deceit running cold in his veins.

"I appreciate the accolade . . ." Drinks poured, Harry handed a chilled glass to the senator from the northeast. "It's certainly a concern," he commented, finally taking a seat in front of his desk, adjacent to Dickson.

A sip. "I'm afraid I have no idea what you're talking about, so, if you have time, I'd like to hear . . ."

With an audible sigh, Harry placed his drink on the small table between them. "Well, it appears there's an undercurrent of . . . well, let's just say there's an undercurrent of unsavory behavior among some of our esteemed colleagues."

"What sort of behavior, Harry? If there's something going on I should know about, I need to know. No sugar coating . . ."

Stanton was quiet for a moment, weighing his options. If what he had to say were true? It would be the biggest political scandal in U.S. history. If not?

He'd look like a fool.

"Keep in mind, Derrick, what I'm about to tell you must remain between us—I know I can trust you, and you'll keep our conversation confidential."

"Thank you, Harry—that means something."

It meant something, alright—it meant Harry Stanton was a moron if he thought anyone in Congress could keep his or her yap shut. "So, what is it you have to tell me?"

With a heavy sigh, Harry Stanton sat back, took a sip, then leveled a serious look at Senator Derrick Dickson. "Five years ago . . ."

Senator Powers tapped his cell screen, fading it to black. "I told you I'd be called back," he told his wife as she stacked dishes in the dishwasher.

"When?"

"Tomorrow . . ."

Susie Powers turned to him, leaning against the counter. "They're not giving you much time . . ."

"Well, something's brewing, that's for sure. Derrick texted me about an hour ago, telling me I needed to get my ass back to Washington."

"No explanation?"

"None."

Again, his wife turned to the dishes. "Did you ask him?"

Jake grinned, loving his wife's no-nonsense way of life. "Nope—I didn't feel like getting into a long, drawn-out conversation. He can be pretty long-winded . . ."

Susie matched his grin. "Do you know a politician who isn't?"

"Point taken. Anyway, I'll try to line up a flight for the morning . . ." With that he headed to the den, Derrick's text front and center in his mind.

Return ASAP—things are about to blow.

CHAPTER 4

*T*me passed.

With several from which to choose, Colbie wrestled with the idea of picking up another investigation, something she really didn't want to do. After returning from Georgia, it felt good to relax in her own home, thoughts seldom returning to her contemplative, soul-searching journey to the Yucatan—something she considered a complete bust. *Maybe I need a shrink,* she thought as she opened a text from Ryan.

Time to talk this week?

Skimming the keys as she typed her response, her face flushed with guilt as she gently told him no. The truth was she didn't want to think about working with Kevin and him again—she wasn't ready and, knowing he wanted her to rejoin their investigation firm, she was beginning to believe doing so was a closed door. But, when considering other avenues, nothing seemed exciting nor worthwhile.

Of course, there was the possibility Colbie believed she was only good at one thing, but, when really thinking about it, she knew that wasn't true. "Colbie Colleen, you can do anything you want in this world, and don't let anyone tell you otherwise," her grandmother told her when she was ten—and, Colbie believed her. It wasn't until a few relationships soured, her confidence tanked, leaving her depleted and discouraged in high school. That's when she discovered solace in her shadow world and, by the time she graduated from college, retreating to it became an all too familiar refrain.

Still, no matter the pull—the desire—on that dreary, frigid fall evening when she could have used a friend, Colbie Colleen refused to succumb to its comfort. Something inexplicable tugged at her thoughts, as if itching to tell her something she needed to figure out for herself.

What, she had no clue.

"Okay—I'm here." Jake Powers threw his camel hair coat on a chair, than sat in the one beside it. "What's so important?"

Dickson sat back, tossing his pen on the desk. "What do you mean?"

"You said things are about to blow! When I left a couple of weeks ago, everything was at a standstill, as usual—so, by the tone of your message, something changed." Jake made little attempt to hide his irritation—Derrick Dickson wasn't one of his favorite people, and the fact Powers lost a good chunk of his time off to answer Dickson's call?

Not happy.

There were, however, other considerations. Colleague backing and promotion were expected, so, when voting rolled around, it was wise to play well with others.

"Remember that conversation I had with Harry several weeks ago?"

"The one when you walked out?"

Dickson nodded. "After giving it some thought, it occurred to me I was a bit hasty—so, I begged his forgiveness, asking him to elaborate."

"On?"

"Why he thinks something is going to happen . . ." Derrick watched his colleague carefully, gauging his reaction. Taking the senator into his confidence was an obvious risk, but one he felt worth taking.

Jake checked his watch—a quarter past the hour. "Okay, Derrick—spit it out. I have another meeting in thirty. . ."

An admonition? Perhaps. Either way, Derrick Dickson wasn't accustomed to being rushed by anyone, let alone a lowly senator from the northwest. In all of his years in Congress, Powers had little to show for his efforts and, in Dickson's mind, that put him smack dab in the middle of the same category as Harry Stanton. "Perhaps, then, we should schedule enough time when you can stay . . ."

Jake eyed him, surging irritation unmistakable. He stood, snatching his jacket from the back of the chair. "Have Constance call my office . . ."

With that he was gone, leaving Derrick Dickson to consider whether he made an egregious error when considering confiding. But, when he thought about it, there was no one else he might possibly trust—everyone else sank to the bottom of his list as a mere crapshoot for keeping their mouths shut. Rendering them unacceptable, he needed someone with whom he could take a formidable stand. Why?

Because two hours of listening to Harry Stanton rocked him to his core.

When Congress wasn't in session, the days seemed more tolerable, somehow—although the politician's life was good for a while, its luster was tarnishing quickly. A simmering discontent percolated just below the surface, giving rise to thoughts of cashing in his political chips. *And, why not*, he thought as he gingerly extracted a piping hot meal from the microwave. *I've done my time . . .*

Minutes later, he kicked off his shoes, propping his feet on the coffee table, waiting for his meal to cool—and, as much as he wished differently, he couldn't get his conversation with Derrick Dickson out of his mind. Obviously, Dickson was itching to tell him what he and Stanton discussed—although, anything close to the truth was questionable, causing Jake to feel it would fall to him to prove or disprove allegations, should they arise. If they did?

Lives would change.

Then, without thinking, his thoughts turned to Colbie Colleen—you know, how odd it was they ran into each other after so many years. Although he'd never admit it to anyone in his current circle, he never quite got over the beautiful redhead after his father was transferred to the coast for work. Although Jake wanted to keep their relationship going, it wasn't to be, his parents never understanding why he was so reluctant to move.

It wasn't only because Colbie was pretty and petite, and he loved the way she looked on his arm—although, that made him feel like a million bucks. No . . . it was something deeper. Something he knew he couldn't share with anyone else.

Something he felt compelled to keep to himself.

"There will, of course, be hell to pay should you confide in anyone about our conversation . . ." Harry stood at the top of the staircase, steadying himself slightly before taking the first step.

Dickson looked at him, noticing the unfamiliar, budding signs of age his colleagues spoke of, but only among themselves. In that moment, there was no question Senator Harry Stanton would be relinquishing his seat sooner than many anticipated. "I haven't said a word, Harry . . ."

"Make sure you don't—dealing with a scandal right now is exactly what I don't need!" With that, the senator placed his hand on the railing, not bothering to bid Dickson an obligatory goodbye as he descended the staircase more careful than usual.

Dickson stood for a moment, thinking, then turned, feeling sightly uncomfortable, the hair on his arms standing at attention. *What the hell* . . . Again, he focused on Harry as he reached the Capitol's main floor. Then, slowly, he glanced up the stairs to the floor above. There, Jake Powers stood . . .

Watching.

Constance Parnell paid close attention as her boss closed his office door gently without saying a word. As he passed her desk, there was little doubt something was off. He'd been particularly irascible over passing weeks, displaying an uncustomary disrespect to her and most of his staff—but, that day?

She wasn't sure what to think.

Until she knocked on his office door only to find him deader than a doornail, sitting erect in his desk chair, a half-eaten ham and cheese sandwich with Italian dressing staining his suit pants.

Well, you can imagine.

Politics were put on hold for the next several hours as medical personnel took care of business, finally passing the senator off to the coroner. By the time Harry Stanton was on his way to the morgue, only a few lingered, chatting quietly. One might surmise they could only speak of the senator's career, and how much he would be missed.

Not so much.

On their minds?

Who would fill dear Harry's seat . . .

"Colbie? It's me—Jake!"

Colbie glanced at her nightstand, the clock cueing her it was too late for anyone one to be calling. "Do you know what time it is?"

Jake chuckled. "I do—and, I'm sorry. But, honestly—I don't think I could have waited until morning."

Although it had been years, she recognized an urgency in his voice. "What can't wait?"

Silence.

"Jake?"

"I know—I'm sorry. But, I think it's better we speak in person . . ."

Immediately, Colbie sat up in bed, switching on the nightstand lamp, her intuition ramping up. "Are you in danger?"

"No—at least, not right now."

"That doesn't sound too encouraging . . ."

Jack paused, again reticent to discuss anything over the airwaves. "I'm planning on coming back to Seattle—will you have time to meet?"

Quickly, Colbie considered her calendar. "When?"

"Day after tomorrow . . ."

"Call me when you get in . . ."

"Still sticking with the hot chocolate, I see . . ." Jake grinned as Colbie took her first sip, closing her eyes for a moment with pure satisfaction. "And, before I forget, thank you for meeting with me on such short notice . . ."

"It's not a problem, but I admit I'm a little more than curious . . ."

"That makes two of us . . ."

Colbie waited as he took a sip of coffee, then sat back in the booth, eyeing a couple as they passed by. As she sat across from him, he felt the same—kind. Compassionate.

Psychic.

"I don't know how to explain it because everything feels as if things are happening away from the mainstream . . ."

"Mainstream politics?"

A nod. "Exactly."

Again, Colbie was quiet, recalling his intuitive abilities when they were in high school. It was something he refused to admit or deny to anyone but her, including his parents. "They'll think I'm nuts," he once told her, asking her to keep his secret.

"Okay—but, you're not really telling me anything. Are you in some sort of trouble?"

Jake smiled, appreciating she thought of such a thing. "No—I'm not in trouble." A pause. "But, a few things have happened . . ." He hesitated, knowing he shouldn't tell her what Derrick Dickson alluded to before poor Harry Stanton cashed in his chips.

But, he would.

Pausing as the server arrived with breakfast, neither said anything other than an appreciative 'thank you' until she was out of earshot. "This looks great," Jake grinned as he took a mouthful of scrambled eggs with fresh salmon and dill. "I miss Seattle food . . ."

Both taking a moment to enjoy their first bites, Colbie finally asked the question he probably couldn't answer. "I feel as if you're questioning someone . . ."

Without looking at her, he nodded, then took another bite. "Keep going . . ."

"It's placing you in a precarious position . . ." She paused, waiting for confirmation or denial. "One possibly costing you your career . . ."

Finally, Jake placed his fork on the side of his plate, wiped his mouth with his napkin, then leaned back in the booth, focusing his attention squarely on her. "So, you can see why I needed to see you right away . . ."

"It's serious, isn't it?"

"Serious enough that I'm not quite certain of my next move . . ." Suddenly, he took another sip of coffee and stood, throwing thirty bucks on the table. "I'll be in touch . . ." Then?

Gone.

Stunned, Colbie watched at he turned briefly to catch her eye as he passed the window, knowing something triggered his leaving. Not quite understanding, she tracked him as he crossed the street, then disappeared into the morning crowd.

Watch your back, she thought, feeling as if Jake Powers were in way over his head. *Watch your back . . .*

CHAPTER 5

*D*errick Dickson pushed open the heavy oak door, scanning the tavern for faces he may recognize—or, who may recognize him. Since it was a Monday, chances were good sycophantic hacks who only dreamed of starring roles in D. C. wouldn't yet be drowning their sorrows for being little more than ordinary. For him?

Timing was everything.

The bartender nodded slightly, directing him to the back table, one reminding Derrick of a vintage movie filled with murder and intrigue. "I don't have much time," he announced as he sat, the man across from him, expressionless. "Make it quick . . ."

"I hardly think you're in a position to be barking orders," the man commented as Dickson stripped off his gloves. "Besides, if you have any interest in what I have to tell you, you'll sit across from me for as long as it takes." An arrogant pause. "Don't you think . . . Derrick?"

With sour distaste rising in his throat, Dickson said nothing.

"I see—well, I suppose it is better for you to remain silent. I can't imagine how that would be any different than your past and present performance in our illustrious senate."

As the senator scrutinized the man, instantly he knew he'd never seen him before—yet, somehow, he had Dickson's personal cell number. "Who are you?" A question most likely to be unanswered, but it was worth a shot.

"My identity is none of your business—all you need to know is I have information."

"For a price, I assume . . ." Dickson didn't take his eyes from the man, noting everything about him—a lanky build, pointy face, and long nose reminded Derrick of Pinocchio.

"Oh, please . . ." A pause. "May I call you Derrick?" Not waiting for Dickson's answer, he continued. "Of course, there's a price—quite a hefty one, too. When compared to others, I mean . . ."

"How do I know you're worth it?"

"You don't—but, I assure you, I can make or break your career. Whether you choose to pay for the luxury of holding on to what you so dearly treasure is completely up to you." Another pause. "Your choice . . ."

Silence.

"So, what will it be, Derrick? Information keeping you from something you'd rather not endure? Or, forever wondering if you could have prevented your demise . . ."

Senator Dickson's eyes narrowed as he stood. "I'll have no part of your extortion—and, I'll be changing my cell." With flair and flourish, he pulled on his gloves. "Don't contact me again . . ."

Chuckling, the man motioned to the newly-emptied seat across from him. "Please sit. I don't think you quite understand, Derrick—would you like me to explain it to you?"

Refusing the offer to again sit across from him, Dickson tugged on his coat, making certain the lapels were straight. "As I said, don't contact me again . . ."

"Well, I apologize for my lack of clarity—it's obvious you don't understand."

"Understand what?"

"The wheels, Derrick—the wheels."

"What wheels?"

The man, too, stood. "I'm surprised I have to tell you, Derrick." A pause. "It's rather disappointing, really . . ."

"Stop wasting my time! What wheels?"

"Why, the wheels you just put in motion . . ."

Early fall transformed into winter, Seattle days dreary and cold, filled with little promise of anything. Colbie didn't hear from Jake again, prompting her to wonder if he were, indeed, in over his head. As much as she didn't want them to, thoughts of getting in touch zipped into her mind and out again, never settling for fear of upsetting . . . well, something.

The whole thing was just flat out weird, she thought, flipping through her high school yearbook. Why she dragged it out of deep storage, she didn't know—but, something was telling her to scrutinize it from cover to cover.

Smiling as she focused on pictures of friends long forgotten, when she landed on a photo of Jake and her at prom, the warmth of youth wrapped her in memories. Although Brian was the man with whom she planned to spend the rest of her life, Jake was the person who completely understood.

Even so, as she drifted from page to page, there was little to help her learn why Jake Powers left their breakfast meeting nearly two months prior without explanation.

Still, she couldn't shake the feeling he needed her help.

Without allowing time to talk herself out of it, she tapped her cell, then waited for the call to connect. Figuring he was embroiled in government business, she left a brief message asking him to get in touch.

Then, she called his wife.

A risky move to be sure, but, since Susie Powers already knew who she was, Colbie figured a call to check on her long-time friend wouldn't be out of line.

Moments later the call connected and, after a brief introduction, both women got down to business. "I don't know why," Colbie began, "but, I have a feeling something isn't right with Jake . . ."

Susie Powers was quiet for a moment, considering whether she should spill her guts about the little she knew. "He's fine—although, he seems a little more stressed than usual. You know . . . political gridlock."

"I can't imagine . . ."

"But, to answer your question, he hasn't mentioned anything specific . . ."

"When was the last time you spoke with him?"

"A couple of nights ago—he said he wouldn't call until tomorrow because of meetings outside of Washington. By the time he could call, it'd be too late . . ."

"His schedule must be hectic . . ."

"It is, but there's something about it he really enjoys. Or, at least he used to . . ."

"What do you mean?"

"Well, you know Jake—even though it's been a long time. He enjoys the debate, and sticking up for those he believes are being wronged . . ."

Colbie laughed. "He was like that in high school, too—always helping someone." She paused, wondering if she should ask her next question, knowing she must. "Does Jake ever mention who gives him trouble?"

"You mean in D.C.?"

"Yes—I know the political scene can be pretty cutthroat, so I'm wondering if someone said something to Jake recently."

"Like what?"

Colbie shook her head, although Susie Powers couldn't see. "That's just it—I don't know." Time for honesty. "I just have a feeling something's wrong . . ."

Silence.

"I'm sorry! I shouldn't have called . . ."

Susie's voice caught as she privately acknowledged Colbie was right. "I'm glad you did . . ."

"I don't like the way things are shaping up . . ." Keith Glidden glanced at his colleague, a sour look pasted on his face. "Who knows who Stanton blabbed to before he croaked? With his mouth, I'm surprised the whole damned Senate doesn't suspect!"

Glaring at him, Dickson didn't like what he saw. The senator many loved to hate dug his own grave when stepping out with a Washington power broker from the other side of the aisle. Those of considerable political experience as well as skilled in surreptitious behavior considered it party treason—and, Derrick Dickson was one of them.

Glidden was, however, necessary.

"Nobody knows anything . . ." Dickson assured him.

It wasn't, however, quite that easy for a man who recognized the stench of corruption. Money, he knew, had its own particular scent, and Derrick Dickson wreaked of it—although, he could say the same for himself. "Who knows?"

"As far as I know, no one . . ."

"Then, how in God's name . . ."

"Did Harry know to talk to me in the first place?"

Glidden nodded.

Dickson said nothing, thinking about a possible course of events changing the way Washington did business—a fact causing more than mere consternation for some. "Because he was arrogant enough to think he had enough clout to shut us down—although he wasn't one hundred percent certain, his accusations were circumspect."

"Obviously, he had no clue you're involved . . ."

"Correct—everything he said was based on supposition. Which is precisely why I wanted to have a conversation with him. I needed to find out how much he knew . . ."

Another glare. "Quite a risk . . ."

"Not really—it was Harry Stanton, after all."

Glidden was silent, mulling over possible repercussions. "Everyone needs to know . . ."

"That I talked to Harry?"

"Yes—if we're to be successful, we need to make certain we know what the other is doing."

While Keith Glidden's suggestion sounded plausible, it was a path Dickson didn't want to entertain. Always a proponent of privacy, the thought of being open and aboveboard was nothing less than abhorrent. "I prefer to keep our conversations private . . ."

Glidden rose, then crossed to Dickson's office door. "Perhaps. For now . . ."

Walker Newton.

A freshly-scrubbed newbie when it came to Washington politics—but, as his mama always taught him, there wasn't anything he couldn't master. Another life lesson she kept sacred? "Do anything you must to make it work, Walker," she told him, her face set with deep, societal defiance. "Anything, at all . . ."

It was that particular bit of wisdom he held dear, and one to which he remained tethered when times got tough. Although his mama departed this world due to what he considered opaque circumstances, he carried with him her strength, resolve, and ability to manipulate. For Walker? It was nothing to turn a conversation in the direction he wanted it to go, sparking a meteoric rise within the ranks of his colleagues much sooner than anyone expected.

By the time Newton stepped into the shoes of his mentor, Carlin Overman—who, unfortunately, took a silenced bullet to the back of his brain three years prior—he felt well-prepared enough to tackle his ultimate goal. His insatiable lust.

Politics.

So, when the perfect opportunity arose to embed with the power mongers within Washington's hallowed halls?

How could he refuse?

One thing led to another and, by the time he strolled the corridors with the best of them, his silent reputation was one of diligence, tenacity, and intimidation. Often hired to bird dog those who might cause irreparable damage to life, limb, or reputation, Walker Newton somehow managed to instill an errant sense of trust with his . . . employers.

Of course, such surveillance was always held close to the vest, only a handful knowing of his true vocation. It was Newton's ability to keep a secret landing his name on certain politicians' lips as an arrogant blackmailer, spy, and enforcer.

Quite the résumé, indeed.

There was, however, a natural fear of discovery, but, with what he charged for clandestine services?

Worth every dime.

You see, Walker Newton was one of those guys who would just as soon shoot your sorry ass as look at you—and, those on Capitol Hill who had reason to know his name, knew it. Seldom did anyone utter his name aloud, and it was only behind a veil of deceit the truth surfaced.

He was, however, more than a little miffed when Derrick Dickson refused his offer which, to him, made no sense. *Surely,* he wondered as he stripped his weapon for a good cleaning, *he must be smarter than that . . .*

A probing question raising considerable doubt.

It was strange—when Colbie clicked off from her conversation with Susie Powers, she felt as if Daria Bendix guided the conversation. *If that's the case,* she thought, *there has to be a connection between her death and Jake Powers . . .*

The more she considered that thought, however, the more absurd it seemed. Since Daria passed, there was no talk of anything other than illness—and, her parents were content with the pneumonia proclamation. Whether such closure were false didn't seem to matter for one reason . . .

They needed to believe.

With that train of thought guiding her, contacting them with questions of possibility seemed not only in bad taste, but cruel, as well. There was, though, no backing off from her promise to Daria—she appeared to Colbie for a reason, and Colbie wasn't about the renege on her promise.

It was then Colbie realized she couldn't conduct any sort of investigation sitting on her couch. It wasn't her style—and, there was no substitute for getting her boots dirty. As much as she wanted to get out of the investigation game, there was always something calling her back—and, when tapped to help, there was no way she would say no.

I promise I'll find out the truth, she silently promised her closest friend. *If something isn't right, I'll be the first to call bullshit . . .*

Snatching her cell from the coffee table, she tapped the screen, her first inclination to text Ryan. But, when she thought about it, doing so might send the wrong message.

Fifteen minutes later?

A flight to the beltway.

CHAPTER 6

Eric Stanton stared at his wife. "Don't you get it, Elaine?"

"Get what, Eric? The fact your father was shooting off his mouth to anyone who'd listen?" She paused, refusing to back down. "Mark my words—they'll come back to haunt us!"

"Oh, for God's sake! Everyone knew Dad was losing it! I doubt anyone paid attention to anything he said . . ."

"Oh, please—no matter what you say, your father had standing until he dropped dead! If you think otherwise, you're dumber than I thought!" With that, Eric Stanton's wife rose, grabbed her coat and headed out the door, leaving him to wonder what the hell just happened.

She was right, of course. There was no telling who—
or how many—Harry told about his suspicions regarding
several of his colleagues—and, it was more than a good bet
a few would take Harry seriously. But, when it came down
to it, there was little Eric Stanton couldn't handle, especially
when it came to his father gaffes as well as occasional faux
pas.

Still—Elaine was right.

Eric grabbed his cell and stylus, tapping on the first
person he put on speed dial. "Just checking in . . ."

"Nothing to report . . ."

Silence for a moment or two as Eric thought about how
to approach his concern. "Have you heard anything?"

The man on the other end said nothing, instantly aware
something wasn't quite right. "What seems to be the issue,
Eric?" Why are you calling?"

"No reason—as the time inches closer, I'm just a little
anxious. That's all . . ."

A chuckle. "Because you're Harry Stanton's son?"

"That's one reason—people expect me to be just like
my father, and that's not the case. Despite our political
differences, however, we had one thing in common . . ."

"Your love of money?"

"Exactly . . ."

"It's a powerful motivator—one bringing men to their
knees if things don't go right."

"That's what I'm afraid of . . ."

"When did you get in?" Jake allowed the server to place their drinks on the table, turning his attention to her. "We'd like to take our time—will you please check back in thirty?"

With a smile and a nod, she agreed, then headed for the kitchen. "She's a happy gal," he commented with a grin.

"Indeed, she is! And, she's pretty good at her job from what I can see . . ." Colbie sat back in the booth, not taking her eyes from her good friend. "So—why the hell did you run out on me at the restaurant?"

Jake laughed, enjoying the familiar, direct approach. "Well—it's a long story."

"I have time . . ."

"Okay—I thought I saw someone I didn't want to see."

"Who?"

"That's just it—I don't know who it is, but, when I laid eyes on him in the restaurant, I got a feeling like never before telling me to get the hell out of there . . ."

Colbie was quiet for a moment. "I'm glad you listened. But, why didn't you get in touch to tell me?"

"Because I think I'm being surveilled—in person, and in my digital communication."

"What? Why?"

"That's what I'm trying to figure out . . ."

"You have no idea?"

Jake shook his head, then took a sip of chardonnay. "It started shortly before I saw you in Seattle . . ."

"Do you think it has anything to do with why you were called back during your break?" A pause. "Who called you?"

"To return to Washington?"

Colbie nodded. "Yes—someone important?"

"Yes—at least in his own mind. Derrick Dickson isn't one of my favorite people, and it wasn't a surprise when it became clear he wanted Harry's clout and respect."

"So, why did he want you to go back?"

"I never did find out—but, something's going on. I can feel it—I saw him talking to Harry Stanton at the Capitol, and Harry didn't seem pleased."

"I've heard the name—didn't he die recently?"

"A couple of months ago—the same day I saw them talking at the top of the steps."

"Did you hear anything?"

Another sip. "Nope. I was watching from the top of the second staircase . . ." Then, a pause. "The hair stood up on the back of my neck . . ."

Immediately, Colbie understood—in their high school days, Jake mentioned several times when he's in the middle of a psychic episode, the hair on his arms and the back of his neck stood at attention. "I remember . . ."

A smile. "I knew you would . . ." Signaling their server, it was time to lighten the mood. "I'm starving . . ." He glanced at her. "What do you feel like having?"

Minutes later, again left to private conversation, Colbie wasn't about to let it go. "So . . . you don't have any idea who was tailing you at the restaurant in Seattle?"

"I'm not sure he was tailing me—it could have been a coincidence, but I doubt it. I've seen him around Washington a few times, and there's something about him that gives me the creeps."

"But, why do you think you're being surveilled? I have a lot of experience in that arena and, usually, it's tough to spot a professional . . ."

"Because I think Derrick and Harry Stanton were . . . well, I'm not sure, but when I saw them talking? They sure as hell weren't planning getting together for a family barbecue."

"Tell me about Derrick Dickson . . ."

"Left of center, but always walking the thin blue line . . ."

Colbie grinned. "In English please—I'm not the political type!"

Jake matched her smile, then topped off her wine glass. "Derrick Dickson is someone who will do anything—say anything—to launch himself to the top of the political heap."

"But, that's politics—always has been, and always will be. You, Jake, were the one to sign on into that world."

He nodded. "True—but, my intentions were pure. I didn't go in automatically jaded . . ."

"Now?"

"Jaded as hell . . ."

By the time Colbie and Jake parted at the restaurant doors, she really didn't know much more than when they first sat down. One thing she did know?

There was a whole lot more to the story.

The only thing bothering her was how Daria Bendix fit into the mix. As far as Colbie knew, she had few political affiliations, if any, and she was in the States for a little rest and relaxation—at least, that's what Janelle told Colbie at the memorial service. *What if that isn't true,* she wondered, pulling slippers from her travel bag—and, for the first time since her best friend passed, Colbie had a feeling there really was much more to the story.

A whole lot more.

Unaccustomed to East Coast time, she glanced at the clock on her nightstand—a little after three. A quick calculation cued her it was midnight in Seattle, and she had plenty of time left to sleep.

Except, she couldn't.

Tucking a couple of pillows under her knees, she propped up against the headboard again checking her cell, noticing a text from Ryan . . .

Something tells me you're on a case!

Colbie smiled, enjoying how he always seemed to know what was going on in her world. Quickly, she tapped in a response, knowing she wouldn't hear until later that morning. Still, as she thought about him, she felt familiar pangs of loneliness.

There was no question Ryan was always there for her and, if she asked, he'd head to D.C. in a heartbeat—Kevin, too. And, if Colbie were honest with herself, she enjoyed the fact he wanted to work together. So did she. But, after their case together in Europe, it was clear Ryan preferred to take their working relationship to a new level. *It's not that I'm not interested*, she thought as her cell screen faded to black. *It just seems . . . disrespectful.*

Suddenly, the screen illuminated with Ryan's response—

Sounds like you have your hands full!
Need help?

Still smiling and without second thought, she typed in her answer . . .

Yes! I'll email you the particulars!

And, that was that.

"Where's Kevin?" Colbie pulled back from Ryan's bear hug, scanning the hotel lobby.

"I tried to let you know, but I was having connection issues—Kevin can't make it. His mom is having surgery, and he wants to be there for her . . ." He held her at arm's length, admiring how she always managed to look great. "I'm starving," he commented, checking his watch. "Hotel, or otherwise?"

Colbie laughed as she realized there was a comfort she felt with Ryan Fitzpatrick—one warm and inviting. "Let's stick to the hotel—how about if we order in?"

"Perfect! I'll check in, and meet you in about forty-five minutes. How about if you take care of room service?"

Plans in motion, they parted, each looking forward to catching up and working together. So, when Ryan walked in her door, kicked off his shoes, and headed for the fridge, Colbie knew nothing changed. "Dinner will be here in a few minutes—in the meantime, I'll fill you in on what I know."

"From your text, that doesn't sound like much . . ."

Colbie parked on the couch, while her business partner downed an entire bottle of water in consecutive gulps. "Thirsty?"

"A little . . ." His boyish grin warming her heart, he opened his laptop, waited a second, then glanced up at her. "So, what are you waiting for?"

"You're right," Colbie laughed. "I'm slacking . . ."

"Damned straight! Okay—who are the main players?"

Colbie flipped through her tablet, landing quickly on the page with names. "There aren't many . . . the only person I've been in contact with is Jake Powers."

Ryan quickly typed in the name, landing on the senator from Seattle. "Close to home—why is he in contact with you?"

"Long story . . ."

From there, Colbie launched into the salient points of what drew her to the nation's capitol. "That's why the only person I've talked to is Jake . . . no one else knows I'm here."

"Or, that you're snooping into their business . . ."

"Exactly—that puts us in an advantageous position, don't you think?"

"Agreed." Thinking of what Colbie just told him, he realized they had less than little to begin driving the investigation. "How about if I start with Derrick Dickson? I can embed somewhere close without being noticed . . ."

"Good—I'll begin with Harry Stanton."

"What about the guy in the restaurant? The one Jake thinks was tailing him . . ."

Colbie was quiet for a moment, thinking. "We don't have any idea of who he is—or, if he were, in fact, surveilling Jake. But, we have to consider Jake's supposition is correct . . ."

"That's right—and, if so, we have our work cut out for us."

Derrick Dickson's daughter stood in front of him, fingers signing her side of the conversation—moments later, he responded, but without words. You see, from the time she was born, Harper Dickson couldn't hear a thing, and it wasn't until she underwent numerous surgeries for conductive hearing loss, did she hear her first sound. They worked—but, not really. To compensate, everyone in Dickson's family learned American Sign Language to communicate flawlessly as Harper struggled to be what she considered 'normal.'

Both laughed, his daughter planting a kiss on his cheek as she headed out the door. "I'll be back soon," she signed with a sweet smile. "See you later . . ."

After a day of in-depth research, Ryan claimed a spot close to the south wing of the Capitol building, far enough removed to not cause suspicion. When he was sixteen, he visited the Capitol only once, yet he clearly recalled the resonance of voices and footsteps as members and staff—all brimming with self-importance—carried out their daily business. To hang out where cameras loomed, however, probably wasn't the best idea, so he camped just below the outside steps, ear buds in to give the impression he was simply . . . there.

By eight o'clock that morning, foot traffic slowed with the exception of a few who were obviously a bit late for work. By ten?

Not a soul . . .

Until Derrick Dickson showed up, glaring at him as if he were breaking some sort of societal law. Ryan smiled, turning his attention again to his laptop, yet watching the senator's every move until out of sight. *Nice guy,* he thought as he typed his notes.

It wasn't until the lunch recess did he have a chance to see who paired up, and who didn't. Instantly recognizing Jake Powers, Ryan took note of who was with him, taking a mental snapshot.

Finally, Derrick Dickson appeared at the top of the concrete steps, talking to a middle-aged woman, his gestures exhibiting dissatifaction about something.

Another mental photo.

With years in the investigation business, the one thing Ryan knew was not to hang around a location for too long for fear of being recognized later. So, as if it were the most natural thing in the world, he waited until Dickson was well on his way before following. Knowing Colbie was only a few blocks away, he sent a quick text to meet him at the restaurant where political folks met, also telling her he'd snag a table.

Experience further told him to keep a quick change of shirts in his backpack—something coming in handy on more than one occasion. Before being seated, he hit the men's room, only to return with a shirt completely different than the one Dickson might recognize.

Within fifteen, the hostess showed Ryan to a table, only feet from Dickson and the woman he was speaking with at the top of the Capitol steps.

Minutes later, Colbie joined him, sliding into the booth while eyeing the chips and salsa. "I see him," she commented as she took a tortilla chip, dipped, then took a bite. "These are good . . ."

Ryan did the same. "He doesn't look any too happy . . ."

Without glancing in the senator's direction, she nodded. "I can feel the energy of the woman from here . . ." A pause, then she placed her napkin on the table. "I'm going to head for the restroom . . ."

"I know what that means!" He laughed, feeling as if they'd never been apart.

Watching her go, there was no doubt she'd return with information of some sort—the restroom excuse always worked and, when coupled with Colbie's innate ability to talk to anyone, no one she approached had any idea she was fishing.

Ten minutes later, she slid in across from him.

"So?" Ryan kept his eyes on her as she glanced at Dickson. "What did you get?"

"Luckily, our hostess was the chatty type. I made it a point to say how wonderful the restaurant was, asking who was who as she pointed out their all-star clientele—at least within political circles."

"Who's the woman?"

"Constance Parnell—she used to be Harry Stanton's secretary until he died."

"Who does she work for now?"

"I asked, but the hostess didn't know—she seemed rather enamored with Dickson, though"

Ryan glanced at the hostess who couldn't be a day over twenty. "I don't know—he doesn't seem her type."

"Maybe—stranger things have happened. But, I agree with you—it feels more like a silly crush."

Again, Ryan glanced at the hostess. "I wonder if politicians have groupies . . ."

At the end of the lunch rush, Colbie and Ryan linked arms as they followed Dickson and Constance Parnell back to the Capitol steps. There, they parted, going their separate ways, agreeing to meet back at the hotel.

Dickson stopped, turning once as if he felt something—or, someone—but, the only thing he saw was Ryan giving Colbie a quick hug, then head down the street.

No one the wiser.

CHAPTER 7

*B*y the end of the week, a taste of spring settled over the beltway, moods of city-goers fluctuating with each rising degree. Elaine Stanton hummed as she prepared canapés for Eric's guests, knowing her true worth to their relationship was her cooking—legend, really. In fact, there was a time she thought about turning her skills into a business, but, upon regaining her sanity, she realized there was no need to go out and make money.

She had plenty.

"Is everything ready," her husband asked as he blew into the kitchen to make certain everything was to his liking. "They'll be here in five," he commented, snagging a canapé from the serving tray. "Well done, Elaine!"

Smiling and with a teasing grin, she shooed him out of the kitchen. "I'll hear them—after everyone's in the library, I'll serve."

With a quick hug and a peck, he left, his mind at ease everything was perfect. Not that it had to be, of course, but it was what his father would've done. What he would've expected. "Always treat guests with respect," he commented when Eric was little more than a boy. "You never know when you'll need them . . ."

And, it was true. As Eric Stanton rose through the ranks as a politician, he made certain to make what money and legacy he so richly deserved work for him. Contacts were of utmost importance, a commodity regarded as gold, and attendance at social events was for only one thing—to make the most of them. Blessed with the gift of B.S., it was nothing to convince people to do as he wanted. You know—a skill, of sorts.

A politician's skills.

Right on time, guests arrived, Eric quickly guiding them to the library, making sure each had a favorite cocktail—even though it was only three o'clock. "Thank you for coming on such short notice," he officially greeted, handing them their drinks. "We have much to discuss . . ."

Derrick Dickson took a sip, followed by an approving side glance at his host. "Such as?"

Hesitating for only an instant, Eric gestured to Constance to make certain she was prepared to take notes. "Are you ready?"

"Yes . . ."

While some might think it odd a private meeting included an administrative assistant, Eric insisted on accurate records. "Fewer opportunities for discord and dissent," he told her when approaching her with the idea. "Plus, you'll be paid handsomely—it's what Father would have wanted."

A powerful persuasion, indeed.

Of course, everyone suspected Constance Parnell probably didn't really understand their discussions—Harry commented more than once she wasn't exactly the sharpest knife in the drawer. But, on the off chance she did, all were convinced they could count on her loyalty . . . couldn't they?

"To our rise, Gentlemen," Eric toasted, lifting his glass high. "Swift and unexpected . . ."

At that moment, Elaine breezed in with elegance and grace, a tray of canapés in each hand, placing them perfectly between her husband's guests, inviting them to enjoy themselves. Then, as any good little servant would do, she excused herself.

The only thing missing was a slight curtsy.

"What are your first impressions of Derrick Dickson, now that you've seen him in person?" Ryan watched as Colbie got comfortable on the couch, then opened her laptop.

"Honestly? Not much . . ."

"Seriously? I think he's an arrogant ass."

"Maybe he is, but the energy from him at the restaurant wasn't negative. In fact, it was just the opposite—especially when he took that call during lunch. Whoever was on the other end was someone close to him . . ."

"I'm looking into his family life right now—but, you probably got more information just from sitting close to the guy!" He glanced up, grinning. "You sure?"

"Of course, I'm sure!" Returning the smile, she, too, focused on her laptop. "He's married to Mindy Prescott, and they have one daughter—Harper."

"That's the article I'm looking at, too. Just from the pics, they seem like a happy family . . ."

"They do—and, I don't have any reason to think they're not. But, there's a woman I'm wondering about—not Dickson's wife."

"Seriously?"

Colbie nodded, her expression serious. "I don't know who it is, but there's something about her I don't trust—obviously, it's just a feeling. I might be wrong . . ."

"I doubt it. Do you know in what context you can't trust her—or, is it an all-around feeling?"

"I'm not sure . . ." She took off her glasses, focusing completely on her partner. "I think we'll just need to keep an eye out, but, whoever she is, I think she knows something."

"Roger that—what about Jake Powers? I mean, I know he's your friend, but I'm not sure where he's going to play into all of this. For now, however, he's one of the good guys . . ."

"Agreed. Even so, I did do a bit of background on him—you know, college, early career—and, everything seemed aboveboard."

"Same here. The only other name we have to go on is Harry Stanton. I scoured the Internet, and it's not an understatement to say he was the most hated man in the Senate—and, that makes me wonder if his son, Eric, is a nut that doesn't fall far from the tree." A pause. "It's times like these I wish I were more politically oriented . . ."

"I know the feeling," Colbie laughed. "My gut's telling me we aren't going to find anything until we start peeling back the layers . . ."

"Okay—how about if I start with Eric Stanton, and you find out what you can about Dickson?"

Finally, by the time Colbie and Ryan were ready to call it a night, both were clear on the following day's schedule, each promising to keep in touch throughout. "I have Stanton's address," he commented, heading for the door. "I'll be on surveillance . . ."

"Watch your back. There's something about Stanton I don't like . . .

"Oh, great! Now you tell me . . ."

"Well, I wasn't exactly sure until about thirty seconds ago—now I am."

Ryan said nothing, turning at the door to look at her.

"You'll be fine! But, like I said . . ."

"I know. Watch my back . . ."

"What about Jake Powers?" As much as Derrick Dickson wanted to let his irritation show, he refused to acquiesce. Then, he turned his attention to his host. "Eric?"

Stanton was quiet for a moment, then focused on Nash Hobbs, the man on whom he relied for his most—probing—information. "What do you think?"

"He's a problem . . ."

"Why? He's never been an issue before when it comes to driving votes . . ." Eric glanced at Dickson, then at the others. "But, if he's an issue . . ."

"I'm telling you, he is—ever since Harry died, there's been talk about Jake's asking questions."

"About?"

"Things he has no business knowing—they're on the QT, of course, but they get back to me."

"What do you have?" Dickson squared his attention directly on his private investigator.

Hobbs placed his cigar in the ashtray, then extracted a small spiral notepad from his shirt pocket. "From Seattle . . ."

"We know that . . ."

Ignoring him, Hobbs continuing to read through his notes to make sure he wasn't missing anything. "Moved to Seattle when he was young . . ."

Dickson shifted in his seat, irritation beginning to creep. "What the hell does that have to do with anything?"

Ignored.

"What else, Hobbs," Eric asked quietly, knowing Nash Hobbs was the finest private investigator in the country.

Their investigator turned to Dickson. "Why is his early life important," he asked, not waiting for an answer. "Only for this reason—his girlfriend back then was none other than Colbie Colleen."

"Who the hell is Colbie Colleen?"

Silence settled over them as Hobbs took advantage of a dramatic pause. "Only the finest, psychic criminal investigator in the country . . ."

CHAPTER 8

That evening after sunset, Colbie stepped into the bathtub, grateful for its soothing relief—although she hadn't mentioned it to Ryan, some days were better than others due to incapacitating lower back pain. That evening?

She couldn't wait to climb into bed.

Bubbles up to her chin, she soaked, her petite frame fitting the tub perfectly. It was the time of day she loved most, allowing her body and mind to relax to a state of meditation, connecting to her spiritual self. To some, it was one of those things people either believed or didn't. To her?

Integral to life.

Closing her eyes, the day cycled through her mind, questions arising about why she and Ryan were in D.C. in the first place. The fact was Colbie had nothing concrete because no one called her to investigate. No one asked her to poke her nose where it didn't belong. But, the thought she couldn't put to rest?

No one wants me here . . .

So, as the day's tension released, she soaked, thinking, unable to shake the feeling she was missing something important when it came to Daria Bendix. As far as she could tell, there was nothing connecting her to anyone in their investigation—and, why would there be?

She spent most of her time in Europe.

Not only that, Daria was the least political person Colbie knew—a fact bringing her to the decision she was barking up the wrong tree trying to find a nonexistent connection. *Maybe,* she thought as she leaned forward to turn on the hot water again, *there isn't a connection, at all. Maybe . . . I'm making up the whole damned thing!*

Guests long gone, Eric Stanton sat in his library as day tipped to twilight, Nash Hobbs's words echoing in his brain. As much as Stanton would've liked to dismiss the thought Jake Powers might become a problem, Eric knew damned well if Hobbs thought there were an issue?

There was an issue.

Okay, Colbie Colleen, let's see who you really are . . .
Booting up his laptop, it took little time to find the psychic
investigator's name in a search—and, after thirty or so
minutes reading about her accomplishments, little doubt
remained. If Jake Powers were stupid enough to get in touch
with her about things he merely suspected?

A compromising situation.

Still, there was no reason to think Powers did such a
foolish thing. When Eric thought about it, before his father's
untimely passing, Jake's name was never mentioned between
them—a sure sign Harry Stanton didn't consider Powers a
threat. The fact was Harry wouldn't invite the lowly senator
to his home for dinner, and certainly not to something as
intimate and cozy as a barbecue on a stifling summer night.

He did have a certain sense of decorum to maintain,
he thought, recalling how his father instilled a sense of
acceptability in his boy.

Eric closed the laptop, a slight smile on his lips. *Even if
it's true,* he thought, *no matter. She's no match for us* . . .

A silent gauntlet?

Perhaps.

Ryan watched as lights flicked off, only a few left on to softly illuminate a room or two—a sure indication the day was winding down. Of course, he really didn't have much time to surveil after his meeting with Colbie, but he figured it was worth the effort. After all, the best things happen after dark, when those choosing to walk within the shadows become emboldened, tossing caution aside for something more . . .

Exciting.

And, so it was for the lady of the house.

For Constance Parnell, approaching fifty was something she didn't care to think about—why should she? She still had her looks and figure and, the way she saw it, she was quite a catch for any man.

Unfortunately, she was the only one who thought so.

One of the things Harry Stanton always confided was he was a lucky man because his assistant would probably be with him forever. "Who'd want her," he laughed, downing a swig of scotch. "Nary a soul . . ."

But, Harry Stanton was wrong.

Someone wanted her . . .

"Did you make a copy," she asked, turning to the man who made all of her dreams a reality.

Interestingly, the thing few knew about Constance was she possessed a healthy lust for adventure—but not, perhaps, the same type of adventure most might consider. No—Constance Parnell wasn't enthralled by the thought of rafting the Green River in Wyoming during peak season, or hang-gliding for the first time. What rang her bell?

Hooking up with Nash Hobbs for a stroll through the seamier side of life.

"You have to ask?"

"Well, you know how I like to run a tight ship," she commented, returning her focus to her laptop. " It's what I do best . . ." Constance glanced at him, paying attention as he snipped the end of a fresh cigar. "I'll drop the thumb drive in the safe deposit box tomorrow . . ."

"Good. We have to be careful . . ."

"Agreed." She paused, thinking for a moment. "What about Colbie Colleen?"

"What about her?"

"Well, for starters, do you really think she's a factor?" She watched as he placed the snipped end of the costly Havana in the ashtray. "I understand your concern, but what does she have to do with anything?"

"That remains to be seen—but, if she comes snooping?" He paused, puffing lightly as he ignited the cigar. "We'll be ready . . ."

He patted the space beside him on the couch. "Won't we?"

Ryan peered through the binos as Elaine Stanton slowly backed out of the garage, its door closed completely by the time she pulled onto the street. Tinted windows coupled with an inky night made it impossible to determine who was driving, but from the way she maneuvered the car?

He knew.

An interesting time of night to be out and about, he thought as he followed from a safe distance. Staying a few cars behind once she turned onto the main road, it was clear Mrs. Stanton knew exactly where she was going, the possibility of a leisurely evening drive taking a back seat. Within fifteen, she pulled up to closed, wrought iron gates, waiting patiently as they slowly opened. A few seconds later?

Surveillance terminated.

It turned out Jake Powers had a propensity for rousting Colbie from a deep sleep. "You awake?"

"I am now . . ."

"Sorry—but, I thought of something that may prove useful in your investigation."

"Well, I'm not sure I'd call it an investigation—neither Ryan nor I know what we're investigating."

"Well, you're the one who decided to jump on a plane to figure it out," Jake shot back, instantly aware it was frustration talking. "I'm sorry—it's been a tough day."

Colbie sat on the side of the bed, slipped on her bathrobe, then made her way to the small kitchenette. "Why? What happened?" Moments later, she plopped on the couch, bottled water in hand.

"Remember the guy in Seattle?"

"The one from the restaurant?"

"One and the same—I could've sworn he was following me."

"When?"

"Tonight—I got home from the Capitol later than usual and, when I got to my front door, I felt as if someone were watching me . . ."

No surprise, Colbie thought, recalling his abilities when he was in high school. "Okay—but, you said it was dark. How do you know it was the same guy?"

"Well . . . I don't, really. But, it felt like the same guy . . ."

Listening carefully, Colbie instantly recognized similar, doubting frustrations he exhibited when they were young. "I understand—but, from what you just said, you didn't get eyes on him—is that right?"

Silence.

"Jake?"

"I'm here—no. You're right—I guess I'm just making something out of nothing."

"I didn't say that—I'm only looking at it from my perspective. I completely understand your feeling someone was watching you. I know exactly what you mean—but, if we don't know who to track, it's next to impossible to find that person."

"I know . . ."

Colbie was quiet for a moment, wanting to help her friend. "How about this—tomorrow evening, Ryan and I will hang out around your place to see if anything unusual happens." A pause. "Did you get a look at the car?"

"That's the weird part . . ."

"What do you mean?"

"There were no cars parked on the street."

"So, you're saying someone was watching you, but not from a vehicle. Someone on foot?"

"Yep—I know it's not much to go on."

"Well, it's better than nothing!" Colbie checked the time on her phone. "Ryan and I plan to meet in the morning, so I'll fill him in on our conversation—then, I'll get in touch." Again, Colbie was quiet for a few seconds, thinking. "Is everything okay in Seattle? With Susie, I mean . . ."

"What makes you ask?"

"I'm not sure—but, I have an unsettled feeling. When was the last time you spoke with her?"

"Tonight—but, everything seemed fine." Jake hesitated as he recalled something his wife mentioned during their conversation. "She did say, though, she got a weird call on her cell . . ."

"What do you mean 'weird?'"

"She told me someone called her by name, and when she acknowledged, there was dead silence . . ."

"Did the call drop?"

"Nope—that's just it. The person was still on the call, just not saying anything—I tried to brush it off, but, honestly, Colbie? There's something about it that doesn't sound right."

"I agree—okay, let me get back to my beauty sleep, and I'll text you when I talk to Ryan."

Moments later they clicked off, both knowing sleep wasn't on the menu.

Not one wink.

CHAPTER 9

A quick breakfast meeting under their belts, Colbie and Ryan agreed to a late-afternoon surveillance of Jake Powers's D.C. apartment building. "I don't know—what bothers me most about the whole thing is his wife . . ."

"You mean that weird call?"

Colbie nodded as she slipped on her jacket. "I've only spoken with her once, but there's no question she's not the type to be concerned over nothing . . ."

"Why don't you call?"

"Maybe I will . . ."

With that, they parted, Colbie's gut beginning to convince her there was more to the mystery man than she initially thought. *If that's the case,* she wondered, *it's time to start where no one else is going to look* . . .

Ever since Harry Stanton dropped dead unceremoniously in his chair with a ham and cheese sandwich in his lap, things weren't the same for Constance Parnell. One would think she'd have a job in a New York minute—but, the truth?

Constance wasn't exactly a likable gal.

In fact, the only reason Harry really kept her working for him for all of those years was because she knew too much. To take a chance on her spilling her guts about the inner workings of his office?

A poor decision, indeed.

So, until Harry's unfortunate demise, Constance's position within the hallowed halls of the Capitol was forever sanctioned. Afterward?

Not really.

Perhaps the likability factor had something to do with the ease with which she slipped into life with Nash Hobbs— much like Constance, he was always perfectly coiffed and dressed as if he were part of the elite. They did, though, seem a rather unlikely couple simply based on his line of work. It was, however, exactly that luring her to a dual life—one lived with an uncustomary simplicity, the other in shadows and purposeful duplicity.

Complicated.

By the time she was on the downhill slide to fifty, one thing became painfully clear—she had nothing to show for her life in governmental service. And, it was around that time she attended a holiday soiree, providing the opportunity to meet Mr. Nash Hobbs—a somewhat stocky, yet striking man who realized a good thing when he saw it.

Well, one thing led to another as it always does, and they soon struck up a mutually beneficial relationship, Constance loving her new life while Hobbs figured out how he could make best use of the situation. It wasn't until he learned of his new paramour's aptitude for electronics did he fully understand how she could be of benefit. "I want to put you in charge of electronic surveillance," he commented casually during dinner at one of the swankiest restaurants in town. "I can't think of anyone better to do the job . . ."

"Are you sure?"

"I wouldn't have brought it up, if I weren't . . ."

And, that was that.

Constance Parnell had a new, after-hours job coupled with benefits not appropriate for discussion at the dinner table.

Life was perfect.

"Not exactly the best place to camp out," Ryan commented as he maneuvered the rented sedan into a parking space across the street from Powers's apartment. "Too much light . . ."

Colbie didn't say anything, scanning the area. "You're lucky to get this spot . . ."

"This is worse than Seattle," he grumbled, squeezing into the only parking space within sight. Cutting the ignition, he placed the binos between them. "I don't know about this— there are a lot of people going up and down this street. If anyone sees us with binoculars . . ."

"You're right. Let's not use them unless we have to— and, only after dark."

Located only a few blocks from the Capitol, somehow, Jake Powers managed to snag one of the premier apartments in the city. Sidewalks with landscaped bushes and trees lined both sides of the street, providing a cozy, nestled feeling— especially when it rained. "It gives me a feeling of home," he told his wife when she visited during a Congress session.

"You can always give up the political life," she teased, the first time she saw it. "You can have all the rain you want back home . . ."

But, for Jake, life was all about community service. Being a politician wasn't about the money, but what he could do for those who needed help. It was a part of his personality Colbie understood, but saw no glimpse of while they were high school sweethearts.

"It'll be dark soon—when does Powers usually head home?"

"Around seven—he said he'd text when he leaves the Capitol."

Ryan said nothing as a couple passed by their car, barely giving them a glance. "At least we don't look suspicious," he commented, grinning.

Just as she was about to respond, Colbie's cell vibrated. "He's on his way—it'll take about ten minutes, door-to-door."

Both sat in silence, each scanning the area time and again, hoping something would cue them about why Jake Powers felt as if someone were watching him. "It's pretty hard to go unnoticed," Ryan commented, "so, if someone were on foot or in a vehicle, . . ."

"Maybe—but, people tend to be in their own little world, especially in a large city. Many never notice what's going on around them and, if they do, they choose not to acknowledge. It's a sorry comment on society . . ."

Again, silence.

"There!" Colbie leaned forward in the passenger's seat. "He's crossing the street . . ."

Ryan made a mental note of people around their target, taking inconspicuous photos with his phone for future reference.

Colbie didn't take her eyes from Jake, noticing her friend's behavior as he approached his building. Suddenly, he stopped, scanning the street in both directions. "He sees or feels something," Colbie commented as she watched, unaware her voice was a whisper.

"It seems so. For a second, I thought he was looking straight at us . . ."

Then, he quickly disappeared through the building's front entrance, leaving Colbie and Ryan to continue their surveillance until midnight. "That's it—I'm ready to call it," Ryan finally commented, stifling a yawn.

"Same here—so, we leave with nothing."

He glanced at her, slightly surprised at her obvious resignation. "Not really—we clearly saw Jake look as if he thought he heard or noticed something."

"True—maybe he thought he was being followed. But, we won't know until morning—I told him we'd be out late, so I'd give him a call after breakfast."

Moments later, Ryan pulled from the curb, unaware of the dark blue sedan keeping close tabs.

He didn't notice a thing.

"Where did you go last night?" Eric Stanton's eyes never left the newspaper, a juice glass poised in his right hand. "It was late . . ."

"Last night," his wife asked, gracefully smearing Hollandaise on her eggs Benedict so it flowed into the nooks and crannies of the English muffin.

"Yes—last night. And, the night before that . . ."

"Good heavens, Eric! Stop using such an accusatory tone—I don't appreciate it!"

"That may be, my dear, but you haven't answered my question . . ."

Suddenly, Elaine threw her napkin on the table as she stood, then left, her husband's arching eyebrows relaxing in due time. *Interesting,* he thought, lifting the juice glass to his lips, yet stopping before a sip. *I think you protest too much, my dear . . .*

"We ended our surveillance around midnight," Colbie informed Jake as she heated water in the micro for hot chocolate. "We didn't see anyone . . ."

"I figured. It was weird, though—I felt the same thing I did before. Like I was being watched . . ."

"I know—Ryan and I noticed it immediately. Did you see anyone?"

"No—it was more like a feeling. You know, like in a scary movie when the heroine knows she's going to buy it right before it happens."

"I know what you mean," Colbie chuckled. "Not quite that dramatic, I assume . . ."

"Maybe not—but, it was still creepy."

The obvious tension in her friend's voice triggered Colbie not to say anything more, prompting her to change the subject. "Have you heard from Susie? Have there been more calls?"

"No—at least, she hasn't mentioned it."

"Good—I'd like you to keep me up to speed on it, though, if you don't mind."

After promising to do just that, Jake clicked off to begin his day, leaving Colbie to think about why he felt as if someone were watching him for the past few nights. *If*, she considered, *someone is keeping track, there has to be a reason why.* A sip of steamy hot chocolate. *And, that's what I intend to find out . . .*

CHAPTER 10

By the time the holidays rolled around, an undercurrent among politicos accelerated as percolating discontent seeped from the Capitol's seams. Seasoned senators and house representatives ramped up dormant battles while stirring the pot with purposeful intent, juxtaposed political agendas more than rankling a few members.

Although there was nothing concrete, word began to circulate concerning certain House representatives attempting to launch their own platform, quietly decrying the status quo was no longer good enough. Nothing new, really, but when word leaked to the media?

Not good.

It was enough of a mess that Eric Stanton chose to take his fury out on the one person closest to him, Elaine taking it as she thought a good wife should. A faulty perception? Of course—one, however, Eric did little to change. Compliance suited him and, should it ever be in dispute, he made certain to set the record straight.

"We're having a meeting," he informed her. "Make sure you have everything ready by six." He hesitated, noticing a slight swelling of her right eye. "And, stay in the kitchen after serving . . ."

Elaine said nothing, tears beginning to swell—if he saw them, however?

Round two.

It was in that moment Elaine Stanton knew she must make a decision. Stay, suffering all the while? Or, steal quietly away in the dead of night, leaving a life of luxury behind?

The fact they were childless made the mere thought of leaving Eric to his own devices somewhat easier—although, truth be told, she enjoyed never having to want for a thing. Was the price too high?

Perhaps.

"What about Aspen? If we make reservations now, we can ski between Christmas and New Year's . . ."

Derrick Dickson's daughter grinned, quickly signing a question. "For the whole week?"

"Yes! For the whole week!" He glanced at his wife. "Well, what do you think?"

"I think you already have your answer," Mindy laughed, loving the relationship between her husband and daughter. "After all, it's where we met Daria!"

Harper grinned, fingers again speaking her words. "That's right!"

So, over pancakes with bacon and eggs, the family decided. "It'll be good to get away," Derrick confided to his wife after their daughter headed to school. He pulled her to him, resting his chin on her head. "I have a feeling shit's going to hit the fan . . ."

Startled, she pulled back to look at him. "What are you talking about? Everything seems to be fine . . ."

"For now, maybe. But, not for long . . ."

"We have a couple of weeks before the holidays," Colbie commented. "If we don't have something concrete by then, I'm not sure we have a case."

"Are you thinking of bagging the whole thing?" Ryan focused on her, knowing she never bailed on an investigation in her life.

"Maybe. Okay—probably not. Still, we're still in the dark about who—if anyone—is keeping an eye on Jake Powers."

"Have you talked to him?"

"No—other than when I briefed him about our surveillance."

"Such that it was . . ."

Colbie was quiet for a minute, thinking of their main characters. "When you first got here, you surveilled Eric Stanton's place, right?"

Ryan nodded and said nothing, knowing she was working through something.

"That's a pretty late hour for someone to be out and about—and, didn't you say his wife drove to a gated community?"

"Yep—she was obviously familiar with it, so my guess is she's been there more than once."

Again, Colbie was silent. "My gut tells me we need to check her out."

"Why?"

"I'm not sure, but, when I think of her, it's not pleasant."

Ryan grinned, then slipped on his shoes. "That's it? It's not pleasant?" A pause. "Maybe she's the woman you don't trust . . ." Seconds later he headed for the door. "What do you want for breakfast?"

"Just a bagel and cream cheese, please . . ."

With that he was out the door, leaving Colbie to stew about Elaine Stanton, uncertain if she had anything at all to do with Jake Powers. *Other than her husband being in the same line of business,* she figured, *probably not . . .*

Within fifteen, Ryan unwrapped two warm bagels, handing Colbie hers with the paper peeled back just enough to get a good bite. "I went with your old standby," he commented, "knowing I couldn't go wrong with smoked salmon and red onion."

So, for the next few minutes they relaxed with their bagels and coffee, Ryan finally announcing he was leaning toward keeping eyes on Elaine for the rest of the day. "I'm going with your gut," he laughed as he finally crammed his bagel wrapper in the trash. "You've been right too many times . . ."

"Good thing I'm not counting," she grinned, opening her laptop. "Check in when you can . . ."

"What about you? What's on tap for your day?"

"I think it's time for Jake to introduce me to the main players, especially Derrick Dickson." A pause. "I'll call Jake in a few to see what he can arrange . . ."

With that, Ryan was out the door, knowing by the time they connected the following day, there'd be plenty to discuss.

Each would have a story to tell.

"Well? Anything?"

"I'm loading it now . . ."

Both watched her laptop screen as images flickered momentarily, each hoping forty-eight hours of surveillance footage would yield something. "This guy's like clockwork," Hobbs commented, watching as Jake Powers hesitated, looking in each direction before unlocking his front door. "What's he looking at?"

Constance said nothing, watching Powers intently. "It's as if he expected to see something—or, someone," she finally commented.

"How well do you know him?"

"Not well—passing acquaintances, really. Harry's office was nowhere near Powers's, so our paths rarely crossed."

"What did Stanton have to say about him?"

"Nothing I ever heard—but, of all things Harry was, he wasn't a blabbermouth."

Hobbs glanced away from the screen, focusing on Constance. "That's not what Dickson says—according to him, Harry wasn't beyond giving away the country's secrets if it behooved his overall agenda."

"Well, Derrick Dickson can think whatever he wants, but, I'm telling you Harry Stanton knew how to keep a secret!"

In that moment, a niggling thought told Nash Hobbs not to pursue the subject. It did make him wonder, though— if Harry Stanton weren't flapping his jaws, who was? Another question? If Harry had no intention of sounding the alarm about their inner circle, why did he make it such a point to have a private chat with Derrick Dickson about changing the course of history? Of course, when the East Coast senator decided it was pertinent to find out what Harry truly had to say, it was more than a bombshell, one requiring a great deal of thought.

And, planning.

Did Dickson tell us the whole story, Hobbs wondered, keeping his eyes glued to Constance's laptop screen.

A question in need of an answer.

"They'll be out of session shortly," Jake's assistant informed Colbie with a smile. "With the holidays coming up, there's a lot to be done!"

"I imagine so!" Colbie scanned the outer office. "I don't know how you do it! I can't imagine keeping track of . . . well, everything!"

"Oh, I'm used to it! Before working with Jake, I worked with Grayson Marshall until he retired, so I guess that counts for knowing the ins and outs . . ."

"What's it like working with so many important people?"

"Important? Well, some of them are—but, for the most part, the senators and representatives are pretty much regular people." A pause. "Like Mr. Powers for instance—he's one of the nicest guys here. There's something different—and, I think I'm pretty lucky to be working with him!"

"I agree! I've known Jake for quite a while, and I think the same thing!"

Just as Jake's assistant was about to comment, he walked in the door with a smile and a hug for his good friend. "Marissa! How are you? It's been a while!"

"It has been—and, I appreciate your giving me a tour! My book will be better for it!" Colbie turned to his assistant. "Thank you for keeping me occupied while I waited . . ." Then, she focused on Jake. "Keep her—she's a gem!"

Seconds later, they were out the door, Colbie whispering praise for his performance. "Perfect—she'll have no idea who I am," she commented, "and, I want to keep it that way."

But, as Jake's assistant watched them leave, there was only one thing on her mind . . .

Marissa? I don't think so . . . That was her first thought. The second? *If Colbie Colleen's here?*

Something's up . . .

"There are a few people I want you to meet—you know, so you can tune in."

"So far, I'm not getting anything—there's a lot of energy in these halls, so it may be difficult to differentiate."

Jake checked his watch, then guided her gently toward Derrick Dickson's office. "So, to review, your name is Marissa Galbraith, and you're a writer—mysteries. Is that right?"

"I think 'political thriller' might get his attention more, don't you think?"

"Either way—just as long as I don't screw it up!"

Within a few minutes, both sat across from Dickson, introductions made. "I have an appointment in ten minutes," Jake commented, turning his attention to Colbie. "Will thirty minutes be enough time for you," he asked, checking his watch. "That'll be close enough to the lunch hour—I'm buying!" He stood, then shook Dickson's hand.

"Perfect," Colbie laughed. "I'll see you in thirty . . ." Watching her friend close the office door, she then focused on Dickson. "If thirty minutes is too long, feel free to kick me out, whenever . . ."

Derrick smiled, enjoying his half hour as the focus of someone's attention. "Oh, I think I can swing it . . ."

"Well, I don't want to take up too much of your time—I know you're a busy man! So, how about if we get to it?" Colbie paused, collecting her thoughts. "As Jake undoubtedly mentioned, I'm writing a political thriller and, since I've never been to the Capitol before, I'm grateful I have a good friend who can show me around. I wanted to feel the environment for myself, rather than simply writing a description based on Internet information."

"You are, indeed, lucky. Jake Powers is a good man, and he's been an asset to our cause . . ."

"Your cause?" Colbie paused, mentally cycling through her list of questions. "What's your cause?"

What an odd question, Dickson thought, not taking his eyes from her. "Well, perhaps, 'cause' isn't quite the right word—what we want is the same as our political opponents."

"And, that is . . ."

"To serve to American people to the best of our abilities."

Colbie scribbled a few notes, then looked at him. "As you might imagine given the genre of my books, I'm fairly well-versed regarding fundamental differences between your colleagues and those across the aisle. But, I'm always curious when something comes up requiring a unified front . . ."

"Meaning?"

"Well, there never seems to be one . . ."

Dickson chuckled, instantly recognizing if Colbie were well-informed, there wouldn't be such a question. "It's not quite as easy as you might think, Ms. Galbraith. There's much to discuss, as well as opinions to discover . . ."

Colbie listened, ignoring his patronizing tone, yet realizing Derrick Dickson was quite a good tap dancer—she wasn't however, going to let him off the hook. "Of course—but, you have to admit, as of late there's been a certain animus between both sides. How can that possibly be good for the people of this country? There's nothing but gridlock at every turn—and, I would certainly think those who are blocking bills and proposals will suffer the consequences when it comes to reelection."

"Perhaps, but, as you might imagine, we always have a little something up our sleeves . . ." As soon as the words left his mouth, Derrick Dickson realized his mistake. Obviously, Colbie Collen knew more about current politics than he initially thought, and it was quickly becoming clear chatting with her might not be the best idea.

"Well, I'm sure we don't know the half of it," Colbie laughed. "I did hear, however, when Senator Stanton passed unexpectedly, there was a concern over a new bill he wanted to present on your party's behalf . . ."

Suddenly, Derrick Dickson stood. "Ms. Galbraith, I'm terribly sorry, but I just realized I have an appointment outside the building in an hour. With today's traffic, I'm afraid I'm needing to leave now in order to make it on time." An insincere pause. "I hope you understand—and, I apologize! My assistant's out with a horrible cold, and I'm left to my own devices for a few days—the truth is I forgot!"

Colbie, too, stood, following his lead. "Of course—I'm just grateful for this little bit of time."

With that, Dickson ushered her from his office. "There's a bench right down the hall . . . I'm afraid I have to lock up."

So, with nothing more than an anemic interview for her efforts, Colbie patiently waited for Jake's return, all the while aware Derrick Dickson didn't feel like answering her question. *You forgot, Mr. Dickson?*

Of course, she already knew the answer . . .

CHAPTER 11

*P*arked at the corner, Ryan's vantage point offered an unobscured sight line to the Stanton estate, its opulence on full display in the midday light. Closed, wrought iron gates delivered their message of privacy, making it clear riffraff wouldn't be tolerated—gates aside, however, it was the vulgar display of wealth he found particularly offensive.

Decorated with dormant holiday lights, it didn't take much of an imagination to envision the estate wrapped in all of its twinkling glory. *It's a stinkin' waste of money*, he thought as he took the binos from the case—and, although wasted money was an issue for him, the Stanton's unapologetic bid for societal attention was more egregious.

For the first few hours? Nothing. Then?

Jackpot.

Elaine Stanton pulled carefully from the oversized garage, her white Mercedes gleaming in a harsh, winter sun as she approached the gates. Waiting as they slowly opened, she checked her makeup in the rear view mirror, then tucked an errant strand of hair behind her ear. Satisfied she met her own standards, she turned right out of the drive, heading the same direction as she did during Ryan's first surveillance.

Her destination, however, wasn't quite so elucidating— the grocery store, exiting thirty minutes later with enough food to feed an army. Of course, someone of her position had access to assistants to do her shopping, but it was the one thing she chose to do herself. The best ingredients were tantamount and, if she couldn't have them, it simply wasn't worth doing.

As she placed her culinary treasures in the trunk of her car, Ryan quickly checked his notes, confirming the aristocratic couple didn't have children. *Expecting guests for dinner tonight,* he wondered as he tailed her back to the estate.

His gut told him it was so.

By the time Elaine pulled into her garage and closed the door, Ryan was clear about the fact it would be a long night— if the Stantons were expecting guests that evening, he sure as hell wanted to know who they were. The issue, however, was who would be first to report a strange vehicle parked just down the block from the estate entrance?

A risk he couldn't take.

Two hours later, he pulled from the curb, aware someone with an active curiosity may be watching. Within twenty, he arrived at the hotel, brought Colbie up to speed, both returning to the Stanton estate in her rental within just shy of an hour. Ryan parked in a different spot where the view to the estate wasn't as good, but enough. "It's almost eight," Colbie commented, never taking her eyes from the street leading to the Stanton's gated entrance. "We might be in for a long wait if they choose to entertain their guests at a time they regard as fashionably late . . ."

"I thought of that—but . . ."

"There! The black sedan!"

Ryan glanced at her, trying not to grin. "That really narrows it down—doesn't everyone in this city have a black sedan? Besides, it looks dark blue to me . . ."

"Okay, blue—but, I'm guessing they're not all meeting at the Stantons. Look!"

Both watched as four vehicles pulled through the estate gates, resembling a presidential motorcade. "I wonder if they're as important as they look," Ryan commented, keeping the binos trained on the circular drive.

"Maybe—but, if we don't find another vantage point, we'll never get a good look at the guest list."

"Agreed . . ." With that, he gave up his spot for another just up the street. "Can you see," he asked, parking, as Colbie kept the binos trained on the circular drive.

"Yes, but everyone's inside—we'll just have to wait."

And, that's the thing about covert surveillance—two results possible, both a crapshoot. That night, however?

Things were going their way.

"They're here—is everything ready?"

"Of course . . ."

Eric glanced at her, smiling, then stood behind her, placing his hands on her hips, nuzzling her neck. "Excellent, my dear. I knew it would be . . ." Then, a slight nip.

"Ow! Eric!"

Paying no mind, he backed away, grabbed a canapé, then headed for the library, Elaine clutching the paring knife in her hand a little tighter, knuckles whitening.

There's a lot to be said for restraint, although it probably does tend to raise one's blood pressure. With nothing but a side glance, Elaine watched her husband blow through the kitchen door with an over-emphasized sense of importance, privately hoping for the day she could effect her own sense of justice. If there were plans to be made, it was obvious to those close to her it was time to start making them.

Everyone knows a simmering pot is bound to boil over, revealing secrets best kept to a precious few.

"I must be getting old," Colbie commented as she shifted her position in the passenger's seat. "Either that, or cars are getting smaller . . ."

"Well, the fact we've been here for nearly four hours might have something to do with it . . ." Ryan watched as she tried to work a kink out of her neck, barely noticing party time at the Stanton's had come to an end. "Hand me the binos," he whispered, seconds later getting a good take on who graced Eric Stanton's dinner table. "Here . . ."

Seconds later, he confirmed what Colbie suspected. "Derrick Dickson—why am I not surprised?"

"Me, neither—I'm beginning to think like you. There's something about that guy . . ."

Neither said anything as they watched the Stantons' guests make their way to their vehicles, then ease through the iron gates. "It sure as hell didn't seem like a jovial parting," Ryan observed, handing the binos to Colbie.

"Agreed . . ."

"Who's the woman?"

"I have no idea—but, I get the feeling she's there with the short guy. A couple?"

"Maybe—but, these guys don't really come across as the couple type."

"He looks familiar, though . . ."

"The short guy? You've seen him before?"

Colbie kept her eyes on the guests. "I'm not sure . . ."

"That means yes."

"Not really!"

"Oh, please—if you say you've seen him before, you've seen him!"

"I didn't say I'd seen him before—I said he seemed familiar."

Ryan knew Colbie well enough to know it was an argument he wasn't meant to win. So, as the last car drove from sight, he pushed the ignition, then fastened his seat belt. "A late-night bite?"

Thinking for a second, she shook her head. "No—something's telling me we should stick around."

"Around here? Everyone's gone!" He glanced at the dashboard clock. "Besides, it's late . . ."

"I know . . ." She glanced at her good friend, then returned her attention to the Stanton's gate and front door. "Humor me?"

With that, Ryan reached into his backpack stashed in the back seat, pulling out two packages of peanut M & Ms. "You had to ask?"

So, for the next hour, they munched, both extolling the virtues of the perfect candy. Suddenly, Colbie straightened, pointing to the gate. "Is that who I think it is?"

Ryan popped the last M & M in his mouth as he pushed the ignition button. "Yep—the one and only Mrs. Eric Stanton. Elaine to some . . ."

After the first few minutes, the happy cooker's destination was clear. "Same as last time," Ryan commented as they drove slowly past the closed gates of a contiguous, prestigious community.

"Have you researched it?"

"The community? No, not yet—now, it's pretty clear the lovely Mrs. Stanton is stepping out."

"Maybe . . ." Colbie scratched a few notes on the piece of paper she stashed in her messenger bag before leaving the hotel. "Tomorrow we find out everything we can about each home."

"Roger that. It shouldn't be too difficult to figure out who's who . . ."

CHAPTER 12

A few weeks off for holiday cheer is nice, but not for everyone—it would probably be only a few days before Colbie was ready to get back to the beltway. Even so, parting at the Sea-Tac Airport, she and Ryan agreed not to be in touch until after the New Year. "We need our time off," Colbie laughed as they waited for their luggage. So, within thirty, they parted ways—both alone.

Each wondering why.

As it turned out, Colbie did little with her free time, Ryan accomplishing the same—but, when they met again in D.C. after the holidays, each carried a fresh perspective. "I couldn't help thinking about the man and woman at

Stanton's," he commented the evening both arrived back at their hotel. "Judging from the other guests, the woman seemed out of place . . ."

Colbie nodded as she dunked a teabag in a hotel mug. "I know what you mean—and, if you recall, before we left for our time off, I thought the guy she was with looked familiar."

"Did you figure it out?"

"Yep—his name is Nash Hobbs."

Ryan waited for her to continue, smiling as he finally realized she was baiting him. "Okay, I'll bite—who's Nash Hobbs?"

"An internationally known private investigator—that's why he looked familiar! I saw his picture in a magazine . . ."

"For?"

"I don't remember—but, I do recall the accompanying article mentioned his part in a high profile case."

Ryan was quiet, Colbie's newfound information hitting its mark. "So, the question becomes why is Mr. Nash Hobbs hobnobbing . . ." He glanced at Colbie, grinning. "Sorry—I couldn't resist . . ."

"Hobnobbing with the likes of Eric Stanton, et al?" A pause. "My best guess is he's working . . ."

Silence.

Finally, Ryan stated what both knew to be true—Nash Hobbs was a player neither considered. With him in the mix?

A new ballgame.

One might think a few weeks of holiday cheer would soothe a battered soul, offering a brief respite from the rigors of daily life—at least, that's what Elaine Stanton's hoped.

Sadly, however, it wasn't to be.

"Drink," Walker asked with a sly smile. "We have plenty of time . . ."

"I'm not in the mood . . ."

"Since when?"

"Since now . . ." Elaine threw him a side glance, her patience at a low ebb. "We have things to discuss . . ."

"By 'things,' I'm guessing you mean your husband . . ."

She stood, smoothing the full skirt of her fifties-style, designer dress. "Of course, I mean Eric!" Suddenly, she straightened, determination obvious. "I don't know how much more I can take . . ."

Walker Newton crossed to her, wrapping her in his arms. "I know—but, it's not the right time."

Tears welling, she pulled back. "When will it be the right time," she asked, an unexpected, snippy anger beginning to rise.

"Soon." A pause. "We have to be patient . . ."

Again, she melded to him, kissing him gently. "Promise?"

"I promise . . ."

"Something doesn't feel right . . ." Eric Stanton got up, crossing to the small wet bar in the library. "Name it . . ."

"Maker's, rocks . . ."

"You're a man of few surprises, my friend!"

Nash Hobbs nodded, knowing it was a compliment alluding to his work. "It pays to know what's coming," he grinned, waiting for his host to raise his glass in a toast. "It keeps me healthy . . ."

"Not to mention, alive." Finally, the ritual. "To everything we must learn . . ."

Silence as the two men took their first sips. "Meaning?" Hobbs placed his glass on the side table, careful to use the provided coaster.

"Like I said—something doesn't feel right."

"Can you be a little more explicit?"

Stanton shook his head. "Not really—it's just a feeling."

"Well, then, I'm afraid I can't be of much help."

Eric stood, paced a few times, then stood in front of the paned glass window, staring at his weather withered front lawn. "When we first banded together with an unbreakable bond—you know, all of us working toward the same end—there was an inexorable trust."

"And, now?"

Eric turned, then took a chair beside Hobbs. "I first felt it over the holiday break . . ."

"Felt what?"

Another sip. "Perhaps I'm wrong—but, I don't think so." A pause. "One of us is lying."

Not a flicker of surprise. Calmly, Hobbs picked up his glass, took a sip, then another, finally placing it again on the table. "A rather serious accusation—care to fill me in on who?"

"That's just it—I don't have any idea. Like I said—it's just a feeling."

"Well, I'm afraid that doesn't give me much to go on," the detective commented, instinctively knowing his plans just changed. "I suppose it's too much to ask what one of us is lying about?"

Stanton stood, indicating to his guest it was time to get to work. "That's your job, don't you think?"

Maneuvering around D.C. was considerably easier by cab and, as Derrick Dickson neared his destination, a prick of concern presented itself. Of course, there was no substantial reason for it, but it was enough to get the senator's attention— since his family's return from Aspen, there was an unsettling in the air at work and home neither his wife nor daughter felt.

Or, if they did, they didn't say anything—but, he doubted it. Still, even if he were the only one to take note, it was a feeling metastasizing into something he couldn't ignore.

Within fifteen, he stood in front of an historic home-turned-office building nearly twenty years prior, grateful for its comforting feel and ambiance. For some odd reason, the second he stepped across the threshold, he felt a sense of peace. *God knows there's not enough of that*, he thought as he climbed the stairs to the third floor.

Five minutes later, he made himself comfortable at a conference table with seven other associates, each with something on his mind—it was no secret their efforts as of late were somewhat thwarted, obstacles at every turn.

"As you know, gentlemen, it's becoming increasingly obvious we're nearing a time of impending crisis . . ." Frank Arlington cleared his throat, privately appreciating the glass of water in front of him.

"Oh, for God's sakes, Frank—you make it sound as if we're on the brink of disaster!" The tallest man at the table sat back, stretching his legs, his cavalier comment receiving little response. Colin O'Meara glanced at his colleagues, their message clear . . .

It wasn't the time.

Derrick Dickson listened, well aware it wasn't the first time the two men clashed—and, the truth was Colin O'Meara was an ass.

He was, however, the best guy for the job.

"We have two months," Dickson commented in an effort to diffuse a rising argument. "That gives us little time . . ."

"Which," Frank continued, "brings me to my reason for calling this impromptu meeting." A slight smile. "It's come to my attention there's rising dissension among the ranks . . ."

"Anyone in particular," Dickson asked.

"Yes—one of your colleagues, I'm afraid." A pause as Arlington thumbed through several sheets of paper on the table in front of him. "Eric Stanton . . ."

That was news.

"How do you know?" O'Meara glanced at Dickson, then focused again on Arlington. "Stanton's always mouthing off about something . . ."

"That may be true, but until now, there's never been cause for concern."

"Why now?"

"Because there's movement in Nevada . . ."

Silence.

"Source?" Colin folded his legs under his chair, then leaned forward, resting his forearms on the conference room table.

"Boots on the ground . . ." Frank glanced at each man. "We need to counter . . ."

"I take it you have something in mind?"

"We know Nash Hobbs is working for Stanton and his group . . ."

"Don't forget Walker Newton . . ."

Arlington nodded. "Indeed—so, we fight fire with fire."

"Spare us the clichés, please." A pause to consider what wasn't obvious. "What's the plan?" O'Meara sat back in his chair, exasperation beginning to show.

"It's simple—we bring in our own."

It was a turn in the conversation Derrick Dickson didn't particularly care for, one likely to place him in the bullseye of confrontation should there be one. "Care to tell us who you have in mind," he asked.

"Colbie Colleen."

"Who the hell is she?"

"The best psychic private investigator in the business." A pause. "You remember the art scam several years back?"

A brief silence as each member of the firm attempted to recall. "Africa," one man asked.

"Exactly—Cape Town. Something to do with Britain, too, I believe . . . at any rate, Colbie Colleen was credited for bringing down the whole damned thing."

Dickson listened, mentally filing everything Frank said. With a private investigator in the mix?

He wasn't thrilled.

Not thrilled, at all . . .

Counterintuitive to usual political machinations, things moved quickly, Colbie and Ryan answering Frank Arlington's call for speedy results. "The good news is we're already on it in some ways," Colbie commented as she and Ryan reviewed the particulars of the case. "The bad news is we're off to Nevada . . ."

"That's bad news?"

"Well . . ."

"Oh, c'mon—where's your sense of adventure?"

Colbie laughed, then plucked a pouch of chicken nuggets from the takeout bag. "Okay, okay!"

"Did you tell Jake?"

"I told him what I could—but, I'm sure he figures there's a lot more to the story."

So, within the next half hour, everything was settled, both flying out on the same flight the following night. "It's a good thing I packed lightly," Ryan commented as they called it a night. "You on the other hand . . ."

Walker Newton watched as Elaine pulled from his drive, wondering how it was she managed to spend time with him on so many occasions. Did her husband suspect? Probably. But, as long as she performed her wifely duties upon his demand from the kitchen to the boudoir, he didn't really care. Certainly, Eric Stanton must've speculated about who caught her eye, but, in the long run, it didn't make much difference—their marriage was clearly defined, and there was no changing it.

And, that was just fine with him.

Such disrespect was intolerable to Eric's mother—Harry's loving and devoted wife for forty-two years—and, she told her son so on several occasions. "You're just like your father," she scolded when commenting on Elaine's swollen eye, "and, that's not a good thing."

Well, that was a shock! It was the first time Eric heard his mother say anything derogatory about his father and, as she continued to spew uncharacteristic epithets, he didn't much like it. "He gave you everything you wanted, didn't he," he screamed as she continued to devalue everything he held politically sacred.

And, there it was—what Karen Stanton had been holding in for forty of their forty-two years together. What she loathed about her husband. How she cringed every time he touched her. How he stole her freedom.

To Eric?

For the first time in his life, he questioned her veracity.

How his mother didn't appreciate everything Harry gave her he simply couldn't understand, and when his wife brought up the same things?

Well, you can imagine that didn't go over to well . . .

As Walker Newton turned out the bedroom light, his cell vibrated on the nightstand, its screen illuminating to alert him of a new text message.

Be in Vegas tomorrow.
Let me know when you land. More then.

Of course, there was no questioning Hobbs about anything—Newton was to do his job, and do it well.

That was it.

Although Colbie told him little about her conversation with Frank Arlington, Jake Powers had no doubt she was heading to Vegas for something other than his own suspicions when it came to several of his esteemed colleagues. Nearly two months in, she had nothing, still refusing to give up.

Maybe Vegas is where she's meant to be, he thought as he flipped through his notes. It wasn't until he got to page three he had a flashing memory of a midnight blue car driving slowly past his building's front door a few days prior. At first, he didn't think anything of it—and, he probably wouldn't have had Colbie not mentioned the vehicles at the Stanton estate the night of their surveillance. "Most of them were black," she commented casually, "and, there was a dark blue one, too . . ."

At the time, their conversation meant nothing—but, in that moment he knew otherwise. Without hesitating, he fired off a text to his friend.

You said there was a blue car at Stanton's.
I think I saw the same one driving past
my building a few nights ago.

Within seconds, Colbie answered, asking several questions, finally ending with a pat on the back for her friend.

This is the first solid link between
you and Eric Stanton! Good work!

A few minutes later, she tossed her cell on the coffee table. "That was interesting . . ."

"What was that about," Ryan asked.

"It was Jake—remember the cars at Stanton's?"

"Yep—you thought all of them were black."

Colbie laughed, knowing he'd never let her forget the night she decided she needed to get her eyes checked on a more regular basis. "Funny. That aside, Jake thinks he saw the same car driving slowly past his building the other evening . . .

"Well, if it is, in fact, the same car, it's the first solid link we have between Jake Powers and Eric Stanton . . ."

"That's what I told him."

"Anything else?"

"No—I asked him to keep his eyes peeled, and to let us know if he sees it again."

Ryan was quiet for a moment, thinking about the only lead they had. "If," he finally commented, "there is a link between Stanton and Jake, it has to be something pretty major."

"Why?"

"You know as well as I cars don't drive slowly past something unless there's interest . . ."

"Well, that's a stretch, don't you think? It could be nothing more than coincidence . . ."

"Is that what you think? Coincidence?"

Colbie shook her head. "Not on your life . . ."

CHAPTER 13

*E*veryone has secrets. You know—something to hide. Something personally private and closely held for fear of discovery.

Costin Dalca was no different.

There is, however, a substantial difference between a secret sparking social embarrassment and one suggesting avoiding the long arm of the law—and, it was the latter that was a concern for the Romanian businessman. "I trust everything is in order," he commented as he prepared to issue final orders. "This shipment is of particular interest . . ."

"Yes—cargo arrives tonight."

"Excellent." Dalca paused. "Time?"

"No later than midnight—I will be here to make certain everything moves forward according to plan."

"And, that is why I trust you, my friend! Never do I worry about complications when you are in charge!" Another pause. "We have visitors arriving, so I am unable to monitor the transfer—but, then, with you in command, my presence is not necessary."

Mihai Bucur grinned, pouring two shots of Dalca's favorite vodka. "Of course, should you find yourself with extra time, we welcome your attendance!" A pause as he capped the bottle, then raised his shot glass. "To us, Costin!"

With a quick, smooth motion, both men downed the drinks, each ready to cap their meeting and move on. "You know what to do," Dalca commented as he grabbed his coat from the back of a broken metal chair. "I, as always, expect to be notified at the conclusion . . ."

"Of course—do not worry! I will take care of everything!"

Dalca headed for the door, footsteps echoing in the empty warehouse. "Make sure you do, my friend . . ."

"Vegas hasn't changed much—except it's kind of sad some of the old greats are no more." Ryan pulled back the drapes in Colbie's hotel room, city lights and marquees advertising what most visitors came to see.

"People, or hotels?" Colbie hung up her trench coat in the small closet, then unlatched her main travel case.

"Both, I guess . . ."

"Well, from what we saw on the way here, I agree with you. But, things change, I suppose . . ."

Ryan turned from the window recognizing the tone in Colbie's voice. "Sorry we came?"

"Sorry? Good heavens, no! We just have a bunch of work to do, and I have a feeling if we don't tackle it now, things will get worse."

"Worse regarding the amount of work? That doesn't sound like you . . ."

"No, silly—I meant I have a feeling things are going to turn in an uncomfortable direction."

Ryan was quiet, Colbie's comment striking a nerve. "I had the same feeling when we stepped off the plane." He paused, then took his laptop from his backpack. "It feels . . ."

"Negative?"

"More than that—different." He didn't look at her, slightly uncomfortable with the conversation. Although he was understanding of Colbie's abilities, when they took a dark turn, he preferred to be somewhere else.

A confession for only his ears.

Colbie sat across from him on the small love seat, laptop and glasses at her side. "I know what you mean . . ." Then, change of subject. "Everything happened so fast, I don't have a solid understanding—or, feeling—about Frank Arlington, so let's start with him."

"Agreed—I did a little research, but not nearly enough."

"And?"

Ryan opened his laptop, waiting only a few seconds until it booted up. A minute later, Arlington's picture was staring back at him. "Okay—Arlington formed the Arlington Group eighteen years back as a think tank comprised of scholars well-versed in terrorism."

"In response to 911?"

"Probably—but, it seems to have morphed into a watchdog organization more than anything else."

Colbie glanced at him, then slipped on her glasses and opened her own laptop. "Watchdog? That certainly takes on a different tone, doesn't it?"

"Explain . . ."

"Well, a watchdog group can be considered an oversight committee of sorts—you know, keeping an eye on those who need careful scrutiny."

"Including politicians?"

"Especially them. It's an interesting question—if that's the case, why would the president of a watchdog group call me personally, requesting I investigate a multi-million dollar company in Vegas?" Colbie paused, thinking. "From what Arlington told me," she finally continued, "we're investigating a major trucking firm based on the south side of the city, owned by Costin Dalca."

"Never heard of him . . ."

"Neither have I—but, according to Arlington, his group suspects a sophisticated dry cleaning business . . ."

"Money laundering?"

Colbie nodded, focusing on her long-time friend. "Maybe. We had zero time to go over my conversation with him before leaving D.C., so I don't have as much info for you as I should. But, between the two of us, we'll be up to speed in a couple of days."

"Doing what we always do?"

"You mean holing up, order room service for two days, and sink our teeth into it?"

"Exactly . . ."

"When's your room going to be ready?"

"A couple of hours . . ."

"Perfect—let's order a late lunch, and get to work!"

Elaine Stanton wasn't a stupid woman—far from it. So, when she realized Walker and her husband were going to be in the same city at the same time, there was considerable cause for concern—far more than she experienced with their being within close proximity to each other in the nation's capitol.

It's probably nothing, she thought as she planned her luncheon menu for a small get-together of Washington wives the following week.

Still . . .

Unable to put her unease to rest, it was then Elaine Stanton broke Walker Newton's cardinal rule . . .

Never contact him while he was working.

It was risky enough to contact him, at all—Eric certainly wasn't above rifling through her belongings, including her phone, to discover what he could only surmise was a suspected truth. Knowing his inquisitive nature, Elaine always made it a point to act with caution—if she didn't?

Well . . . you know.

Pulling her cell from her apron pocket, her delicate fingers lightly touched the keys as she tapped in a message, sending it without a second thought. *If there's something to worry about, he'll tell me,* she promised herself, plucking ingredients for a cloud-like pate choux from the pantry shelf.

By the end of the day?

Nothing.

Walker Newton smiled, his gleaming teeth the perfect accoutrements to a snappy, polished appearance. When only a boy, his mama stressed the importance of looking like he hailed from money, and it was advice he never forgot—even when he had plenty of his own. Tall and lanky with a body made for expensive clothes, Walker turned more than one head when walking down the street—and, he knew it.

Flashing his pearly whites, he extended his hand. "Mr. Dalca! We meet again!"

"Indeed, Mr. Walker! I hope your flight was as pleasant as possible . . ." Costin Dalca flashed a smile of his own, teeth stained by years of tobacco.

For one who wasn't particularly fond of pleasantries, Walker treated his mark as an old friend. "As nice as a cross-country flight can be, I suppose!" Then, the purported reason for his visit. "I assume everything is under control?"

He smiled inwardly, knowing he asked the ubiquitous, stupid question—if everything were under control, he wouldn't be there. Nash Hobbs wasn't the type of guy to send Walker Newton into an inflammatory situation without doing his homework—and, if Eric Stanton gave the word?

He expected results.

There was a time, of course, Hobbs did the exhausting legwork himself, taking comfort in the pleasure it offered. Never did he feel it was too much—until his heart decided otherwise. A scare to be sure, targeted to encourage a different way of doing business. Shedding a bit of excess weight would have been wise, as well, but doing so wasn't an attractive-enough allure. So, when Walker Newton presented himself as the perfect opportunity to make a lifestyle change, who was he to say no?

"As you know, I'll be at the transfer . . ." Walker stripped off his driving gloves, holding them in his left hand.

Dalca remained silent for a few seconds, thoughts tap dancing around possibilities—mainly, what could and would go wrong. "Actually, Mr. Newton, I didn't know. Of course, there is no issue—however, my partner will be overseeing the transition. Unfortunately, I have a pressing business matter I must attend to . . ."

First red flag.

Naturally, it would have been in poor taste to question Dalca further—such conversations should never happen in front of others just in case attitude adjustments became necessary. "I completely understand, Costin. Your man? What's his name? I'm sure you told me before, but sometimes I forget . . ."

"Mihai—Mihai Bucur. Next to me, he is the best in the business!"

"Excellent!" Newton again extended his hand. "Please tell Mr. Bucur I'll arrive at the warehouse at midnight—no sense in being late now, is there?" Another smile. "Perhaps, we can meet sometime tomorrow . . ."

"I am sorry, Mr. Newton, but your visit couldn't have come at a busier time. Another day, perhaps?" An insincere apology? No doubt.

Second red flag.

It was certainly enough for Walker Newton to make a mental note to keep track of Mr. Dalca's whereabouts. Hobbs already put a bug in his ear that things might become a little—sticky—should Dalca prove to be a problem. And, with two red flags against him?

Well, you know what they say about the third one's a charm . . .

CHAPTER 14

One thing Eric Stanton loved? The courtroom. Any courtroom. It was much like a stage and, from the time he was old enough to always place first in his high school debate club events, thoughts of being a politician graced his dreams. Of course, having an old man already in the biz didn't hurt—many considered watching Harry in action a sight to behold, carefully training his boy in the ways of the political world.

Although trust was normally regarded a necessary undercurrent in his family, it never really played a part in anything Eric did from the time he graduated high school to the present. It was an aspect of their family dynamic his mother despised, yet she was always careful to keep opinions to herself—and, as long as she did?

Peace, tranquility, and no black eyes.

Harry, too, was anything but trustworthy, a trait his son dutifully carried with a certain amount of pride. When a young lady—Harry called her a 'gold-digging tart'—accused his son of fatherhood shortly after Halloween two decades prior, only a select few within the Stanton social circle had any idea of such a false atrocity. Naturally, all rumors and gossip were quashed by the heavyweight politico no one chose to confront. Not only that, no one had the guts to call Harry Stanton exactly what he was . . .

A bald-faced liar.

Due to his father's silver tongue, what could've turned out to be a career-ending, unfortunate mistake—exactly what Eric and his father considered it to be—morphed into something making the Stantons look like saints. Everything hush-hush, there was never to be a new matriarch or patriarch born into their family—at least, not if they could help it. All the while, Mama Stanton looked the other way, refusing to take part in any conversation that could, possibly, place her in a precarious position, which was, probably, a wise choice.

For the filthy rich, money carried on its own, private conversations, and it wasn't the first time Eric needed his father's pecuniary assistance. Harry's son was, after all, a Stanton, and it was up to Harry to ensure any future, untenable situation also needed to turn out to his benefit. Some say there was a private fund set aside for such an emergency, although who really knows?

One thing was for sure—Eric Stanton would never need to defend himself without the power of his father at his side.

Harry made certain of it.

Born into a family of questionable ethics, it was no wonder Eric possessed a staunch and healthy lack-of-veracity trait undoubtedly passed down from his father. So, when Eric showed up at the trucking company precisely at eleven o'clock that night to oversee operations as a representative of monetary interests, Mihai Bucur wasn't exactly thrilled, obvious despite Bucur's slobbering, false plaudits.

Did Eric know Nash Hobbs sent Walker Newton to keep tabs on him?

Nope.

A purposeful omission?

Indeed.

Even so, as reckless as Hobbs's move was, there was something about Eric Stanton's recent behavior raising more than one concern, requiring clandestine action. Elaine's efforts to camouflage her injuries was less than successful, and anyone who didn't see or understand what was happening behind closed doors was an idiot—at least, that's what Hobbs thought.

So, what did Eric Stanton's barbaric behavior toward his wife have to do with sending Walker Newton to Vegas to keep an eye on him? One thing . . .

Once a liar, always a liar.

No one knew Nash Hobbs didn't trust Harry's boy as far as he could throw him—in his personal life, or business. If the nut fell anywhere close to the tree, Eric was surely as crooked as his dad, and his dad before him.

Strong genes.

Another blatant truth? If one person screwed up their plans, everyone would pay—a situation that simply couldn't be allowed to fester. No one else in their circle knew—except for Constance—of Eric Stanton's suspected duplicity regarding their group, and she was instrumental in whatever measures Hobbs chose to take. At the least, placing Walker Newton in Vegas to surveil—let's call it what it was—Eric Stanton was a precautionary commitment. Anything else?

A situation to deal with at a later time.

"This is it . . ." Colbie pointed to a large sign with a giant arrow aimed toward People's First Delivery. "The best trucking company in Nevada . . ."

"At least they're humble . . ." Ryan looked both ways before turning left into paved parking lot with another sign pointing toward the main door to the office. "The usual?"

Colbie nodded. "We're married, and we're moving to Phoenix . . ." She paused, scanning the parking lot and adjacent buildings. "Hold on a sec—I want to see if I sense anything."

Nothing.

A few minutes later, they stood at the front counter, Jessica smiling proudly as she greeted them. "Welcome to People's First Delivery! How can I help?"

Ryan's taking the lead to keep the lovely Jessica occupied while Colbie did her thing proved a simple task. "We've only been in Vegas for a few years," he commented. "But, I'm getting transferred, and we need something quickly." An engaging smile. "Is that something you can do?"

"Why, that's what we do best!"

From there, they were off and running as Colbie took mental note of everything on the walls, desks, and any paperwork she could spy as she slowly ambled about the office. Finally, she made her way again through the front door. "You make the arrangements," she called to Ryan with a wave. "I'll meet you at the car!" A ruse, naturally, one allowing her the opportunity to stroll where she could without raising suspicion.

As she crossed the threshold, to her left stood three steel buildings and, from what she could see, one was a maintenance garage, another for loading cargo. The third?

Not sure.

One thing for certain was it cost a wad of cash to keep something so large running efficiently.

Watching as two moving vans jockeyed into position in front of a massive dock, a small crew of men waited to begin loading. As soon as the semi came to a stop, one man swung open the rears doors, the others disappearing into the warehouse before returning with someone's treasures.

"You ready?" Ryan knew she didn't hear him, offering the perfect opportunity to scare the livin' daylights out of her.

He was right.

"Ryan!"

A grin. "I couldn't resist . . ."

They stood together, watching the orchestration of moving vans maneuvering into place, waiting their turn. "It's quite the operation, isn't it," Colbie asked, shielding her eyes from the sun with her hand.

"That's an understatement—these guys are good!"

"I'm guessing Costin Dalca runs a tight ship . . ."

Ryan agreed as they headed back to their car. "Did you pick up on anything," he asked as he buckled his seatbelt.

"Not really—although, I wonder what's in that third building." She pointed as he slowly backed out of the parking space. "There's a lot of activity in the other buildings, but that one feels like a ghost town . . ."

"Maybe Dalca doesn't use it . . ."

Colbie shook her head. "I doubt it—with an operation this big? He'd make use of every inch . . ."

"True . . ."

"What about Jessica? Where did you leave it with her?"

Ryan glanced both ways before turning into traffic, then eased onto the highway. "I said I'd talk things over with you, then get back in a day or two . . ."

"Perfect!" A pause. "Did you see that guy who was walking toward the third building as we pulled out?"

"No—not really, but I wasn't paying too much attention. What about him?"

Colbie didn't say anything for a minute, thinking she recognized the tall, lanky man. "I'm not sure, but he looked familiar?"

"From where?"

"D.C."

Ryan glanced at her. "I'm not sure I like the sound of that . . ."

Colbie turned in her seat so she could see him without straining her neck. "Or, maybe we do . . ."

When in Seattle, one thing Jake Powers enjoyed was standing in front of the big picture window in his living room, watching a soothing rain. In D.C.? Same thing, only he didn't have a stunning picture window in his small apartment. So, he stood on his tiny balcony against the sliding glass door to ensure not getting wet—although, that probably would've been okay, too.

A cup of decaf in hand, he watched as cars spotted parking spaces, several circling the block making certain there wasn't one closer. It was then he spotted the dark blue sedan parked far enough down the block as if to not raise anyone's suspicion. Still, he took note, knowing it could be something . . .

Or, nothing.

But, it wasn't until the following morning when he noticed Constance Parnell pull into a parking garage not far from the Capitol, did he put two and two together.

Then, he called Colbie.

Costin Dalca sat back in his office chair, glasses resting far down on his nose so he could peer over their rims as he stared at surveillance footage from the previous day—usually, there was nothing of interest. That day?

Antennae raised.

"Jessica! Come in here!"

At the sound of her boss's voice, Jessica's smile faded, knowing his temper. Without hesitation, she put aside her work, then headed to his office. "Yes?"

"Who are these people?" He gestured for her to look at his computer monitor.

"Mr. and Mrs. Blickenstaff—he just got transferred to Phoenix, and they wanted to know how fast we can get them moved." She glanced at her boss. "Why? Is something wrong?"

Not taking his eyes from the screen, Costin Dalca couldn't shake the feeling things were about to change—and, the people on his computer monitor would have something to do with it. "No." A pause. "What about the woman? Why did she walk out the door?"

"I have no idea—I didn't talk to her, at all. All I heard her say was she'd leave things to her husband, and she'd meet him back at the car. That's it . . ."

"Did you get contract?" Most times, Costin Dalca spoke excellent English—when he was unhappy?

Not so much.

Jessica shook her head. "No—he said he'll let me know in a couple of days."

Silence.

Then, a dismissive wave. "Go . . ."

"Everything went according to plan, Costin!" Mihai Bucur raised his glass for a celebratory toast. "Things are good, my friend!"

Costin Dalca, however, wasn't so sure. "We must increase our security," he ordered, completely disinterested in joining his friend for the toast. "Top of the line . . ."

Bucur placed his shot glass on Dalca's desk, instant concern etching his face "What is wrong?"

A moment's silence. "Perhaps nothing—but, I do not want to be in an uncomfortable position."

Mihai knew better than to press. "I will make certain it is installed by the end of the week."

"Sooner!"

Drink still on Costin's desk, Bucur turned, heading for the door—but, before crossing the threshold, he turned. "If there is something I can do, my friend, all you have to do is ask. And, as for the security, consider it done . . ."

With that, he left, closing the door to leave Costin Dalca to his own thoughts.

His own demons.

It had been a while since Colbie managed to snag a good night's sleep, the results of which were beginning to take their toll. Plagued with dreams and images she didn't understand, upon waking each morning, her energy wasn't as it should be, an uncustomary heaviness keeping her under its thumb.

After a quick debrief when returning from People's First Delivery, Colbie kicked Ryan out, telling him she needed her beauty sleep—what she really needed, however, was time with her intuition. Something was bugging her about the moving company, and she hoped to gain additional information from her guides—and, that's exactly what she got as she relaxed on the hotel suite's couch.

Once again, as her meditation deepened, Daria appeared to her friend, hoping to point her in the right direction, no longer communicating with her hands—it was her voice Colbie heard. "You're close. Aspen. Betrayal." Then?

Vanished.

Instantly, Colbie opened her eyes, knowing her friend was leading her in the investigation. *But, why Aspen,* she wondered, as she scribbled notes on the pad she kept on the end table.

Promising to go through them from the beginning of her investigation in the morning, she finally drifted into uncomfortable slumber, instinctively knowing to watch her back.

To keep her eyes peeled.

CHAPTER 15

*I*t wasn't often Frank Arlington stepped out early in the morning to meet anyone, the damp and chill of sunrise in late winter not his thing. Yes, there were times when he had to acquiesce, but he carried enough clout so those who needed a fraction of his time could only be granted an audience on his terms, as well as at his designated time and location. To many?

The guy was an ass.

Arlington watched his business partner slather butter and jam on a piece of toast, place it on his plate, then sit back in the booth, perplexed. "Okay," his partner commented, "I'm here. What's so important we couldn't discuss it in the office at a more decent hour?"

"Privacy. What I have to discuss requires the utmost discretion . . ."

Not quite what Joe Bledsoe expected. "That sounds serious . . ." He was accustomed to private discussions with his partner, but rarely did they meet in a crowded restaurant for anything, let alone a discussion requiring confidentiality. "I find it interesting, however, you chose this particular environment—care to fill me in?"

Arlington took a sip of coffee, then patted his lips with a starched, white linen napkin. "It's simple—no one's listening."

Bledsoe said nothing for a moment, weighing Frank's words. "Are you saying," he finally asked, "we have a traitor in our midst?"

"Perhaps—we'll soon find out. But, I'm quite certain Derrick Dickson isn't as popular as he thinks he is . . ."

"Meaning?"

A pause. "Meaning, I overheard a conversation I had no business hearing. But, I'm glad I did . . ." Arlington glanced at patrons closest to their table, making certain all were engaged in their own lives.

"Between?"

"Nash Hobbs, and the woman who worked for Harry Stanton . . ."

"Constance Parnell?"

A nod.

Again, Joe Bledsoe was quiet, thinking, before asking the obvious question. "Where?"

"The Beltway Tavern. I was seated with my back to them, neither seeming to pay attention to whom may be listening. A rookie move . . ."

"And, the topic was . . ."

"Derrick Dickson. From what I gathered, Hobbs is investigating a certain group of people for Stanton . . ."

"Which group?"

"Us."

Bledsoe didn't take his eyes from Frank's. "They know?"

"They obviously know something . . ."

"Have you talked to Derrick? Does he know his cover's blown?"

Frank shook his head. "I wanted to talk to you first . . ."

"Any idea of how they found out?"

"No—but, I'm doing a sweep first thing this morning. If we're being surveilled, our boys will find it."

"Or, them—plural."

"Exactly."

"We can't drop everything here and head to Aspen," Ryan commented as Colbie placed a cup of coffee on the table beside him. "Thanks . . ."

"I know! That's what makes this so frustrating! If Daria could talk to me all this time, why did she use sign language during her first visits?" A pause. "That makes absolutely no sense to me . . ."

"Well, it obviously means something, don't you think?"

Colbie agreed. "Let's wrap up here as quickly as we can, and hit Aspen on the way back to D.C.—it's not a long flight from Denver."

"You make it sound as if we'll be out of here in a few days. Somehow, I don't think that's the case . . ." He turned his laptop toward her, so she could see the screen.

As she read the headline in Vegas's online newspaper, her chin dropped. "Are you serious?"

Ryan repositioned the screen so he could read. "It's him—Costin Dalca of People's First Delivery. His partner found him last night, double tapped, in Dalca's bathroom."

"At work?"

"No—his home."

Quiet for several moments, Colbie mentally cycled through their time at the trucking company. "I knew something felt off . . ."

"When?"

"At the trucking company—that third building. I'd love to get in there, if we can."

"Maybe before last night that would've been possible, but now? Somehow I doubt it . . ."

Colbie nodded. "I know—cops will be everywhere." She paused, cycling through their visit to the trucking company. "Because Dalca was murdered at home, someone sure as hell was familiar enough to know the layout."

"Especially, the master bathroom—most visitors don't have the privilege of seeing such personal things."

"Agreed."

"So? What do you want to do?"

Silent for a moment or two, Colbie finally made a decision. "We head for Aspen—I don't want cops to get wind of us." A pause. "But, before we do, I think I need to talk to Arlington . . ."

"My guess is he probably already knows about Dalca."

"Same here, but I think it's time Frank Arlington and I had a little chat. I don't like being in the dark, and I haven't heard from him since we arrived . . ."

"Did you update him on our visit to the trucking company?"

"Yes—nothing in return."

"What if he wants us to stay?"

"Well, then . . ."

Colbie glanced at him, then focused again on her notes. "If that happens, I'll bow out. Something about this whole thing stinks, and Dalca's murder is only the beginning . . ."

As much as Colbie wasn't a fan of discussing the nature of an investigation in front of someone she didn't know, when Frank Arlington agreed to a conversation, there was one caveat—Joe Bledsoe would be listening. Even so, there was nothing she could do, but execute the salient points of her conversation with Arlington, hoping he'd tell her what she wanted to know. Was she counting on it?

Nope.

Prelim introductions under their belts, Colbie took the lead. "As I'm sure you're aware, Mr. Arlington, Costin Dalca took two bullets to the back of the head sometime between midnight and seven this morning . . ."

"We are aware." Arlington glanced at Bledsoe. "Is that the reason for your call? To tell us something we already know?"

His was a tone Colbie didn't appreciate, immediately placing her on defense—an uncustomary position for someone of her experience. "Of course not—but, if I may be blunt, I get the feeling there's something we should know. Something you prefer not to mention . . ."

"And, just what would that be, Ms. Colleen?" Joe Bledsoe's tone matched his partner's, further rankling their private investigator. It was no secret Bledsoe wasn't exactly on board with Arlington's decision to hire her—to his thinking, it would've been nice to be consulted.

"There's a third building at People's First Delivery—one that appears empty."

"Why would an empty building matter to us?"

"That's what I'm asking you, Mr. Bledsoe—and, I suggest you speak the truth. As I'm sure Mr. Arlington told you, the reason I'm successful in what I do is because of my ability to cut through the bullshit."

A bold move?

Perhaps.

Joe Bledsoe shifted in his chair, a slow, creeping anger taking root. "Bullshit?"

"Exactly—as covert as you think you are, it's a mistake to keep me out of the loop."

"Is that a threat, Ms Colleen?" Frank again glanced at his partner, then again focused on his cell placed between him and Bledsoe.

"A threat?" Colbie chuckled, knowing she was getting to them. As soon as the call connected several minutes earlier, there was no doubt they were using her—for what, she didn't know. "Good heavens, no! It's simply time for you to be upfront with why I'm in Las Vegas, and why Costin Dalca was murdered . . ."

"I assure you . . ."

"Please—don't insult me, Mr. Arlington. If you're not going to be truthful, then I'm afraid I must remove myself from the case. You'll receive my invoice for final services within the hour . . ."

A pregnant pause.

"Well, Mr Arlington? How should we proceed? I'm good either way . . ."

"Alright, Ms. Colleen—but, what we're about to tell you is of the utmost confidentiality. Should anyone discover our conversation? I think it's safe to say your life will never be the same . . ."

Elaine's eyes filled with tears as she listened, never thinking she would be on the receiving end of verbal abuse much like her husband's. "I didn't mean . . ."

A fresh round of blubbering.

"The one thing I told you was to never call me when I'm working a case! Is that so difficult to understand?"

"No . . ."

In that moment, Walker Newton considered whether Elaine Stanton were a liability—if so, it was something Hobbs needed to know.

As he listened to her blow her nose, irritation burrowed in, patience quickly tanking to zero. "For God's sake, Elaine! Stop sniveling!"

"I'm sorry . . ."

If only she could see the sneer crossing his face—it might've changed her perspective. As it was, Elaine Stanton was reduced to nothing.

Again.

Colbie clicked off, her expression an instant concern. "Well? What did he say," Ryan asked, closing his laptop so he could focus on nothing but her.

"I'm not sure I know where to begin . . ."

Another close look at his friend, and Ryan instantly headed for the kitchenette for a bottle of water. Seconds later, he unscrewed the cap, handing it to her. "Take your time . . ."

Accepting it, Colbie leaned back on the couch. "You're never going to believe it . . ." A sip. "If I knew then what I know now, I'm not sure I would've accepted the case."

"Okay—don't keep me in suspense? What the hell is going on?"

"Like I said, you're never going to believe it . . ."

CHAPTER 16

*E*laine folded her handkerchief gently, then tucked it in her apron pocket, patting it three times to ensure its safety. Drying tears staining her cheeks, she sat in front of the bay window in the sun's waning light, thoughts filled with possible options. It was clear she had a decision to make, but such a task wasn't in her wheelhouse, the mere thought of it terrifying. Since she tethered herself to Eric years ago, the need for making decisions regarding her life lessened until, finally, there was no need, at all. It was, unfortunately, a situation she silently abhorred, but could do nothing about.

Until that moment.

As street lights flickered on like fireflies embarking on nightly journeys, Elaine Stanton stood, her face set with a confidence rarely displayed. *It's time*, she thought as she headed to the kitchen.

It's time . . .

Jake Powers sat back in his chair, listening to a colleague on the other side of the aisle wax on endlessly about something few cared to discuss—a moot point. Even so, it was his job to listen, his thoughts often turning to Colbie and her investigation. Although unable to shake the idea his uneasiness over the prior few months was connected to her trip to Vegas, there was something else occupying his thoughts.

Constance Parnell.

Since Harry Stanton dropped dead, it was a normal assumption she'd continue working within the confines of the Capitol, guiding whomever in the ways of politics. After all, she was a fixture, and the thought of her not being around seemed off.

At least, that's what Jake thought. *There are plenty who'd jump at the chance to snatch her up*, he thought as his colleague droned on. *And, what the hell was she doing at the Capitol if she no longer works here?*

Of course, it made perfect sense she'd show up every once in a while, but, since he saw her car pull into the parking garage?

Something gnawed at him.

So, with such thoughts darting in and out, it was serendipitous when he spied the lovely Ms. Parnell as the Senate broke for lunch. Avoiding anyone who might possibly take him from his target, he followed as she made her way to a small restaurant a few blocks to the north. Minutes later, she was seated, obviously waiting for someone.

Jake watched from across the street as his assistant and her husband stood for a moment at the front door of the same restaurant as she rifled through her handbag, then entered.

Minutes later, Jake stood at their table. "Mind if I join you," he asked, keeping his eye on Constance while taking a seat. "I don't feel like eating alone!"

Graciously welcomed, he glanced at the menu, then again at Parnell just as a stout, fashionably dressed man joined her, giving her a loving peck. His back to Jake, the senator didn't get a good look—until they left together not quite an hour later. Then?

A light bulb moment.

Eric Stanton glared at Mihai Bucur, sparking anger guiding every word. "It's clear we have a problem, Mr. Bucur—one that must be addressed immediately."

"Please—call me Mihai."

Stanton paused, refusing to take his eyes from the man seated behind a chaotic desk. "As I said, Mr. Bucur, we have a problem . . ."

"If you're referring to Costin . . ."

"What else? Considering my investment, I'm sure you understand my concern—there can be no interruption."

Bucur nodded. "Everything is proceeding as planned—the second shipment is tonight."

Eric said nothing, weighing his next move, knowing it was never wise to interfere—yet, with Costin Dalca out of the picture, it was in his best interest to keep track of his investments. "At midnight?"

"No—later. Two . . ."

"Why so late?"

"As you know, Costin was not a predictable man . . ."

So, as the two men stared at each other, both refusing to show weakness, Eric Stanton had a decision to make. Risk life and limb by showing up at a party to which he wasn't invited? Or, shrink into the shadows, keeping a wary eye?

Undecided and without comment, he headed for the side door facing the alley and stepped into the late-afternoon sun, leaving him uncharacteristically exposed.

Perhaps not the brightest move.

"Is that who I think it is?" Colbie adjusted the binos slightly as she focused on the alley. "Holy shit!" Quickly, she handed the binoculars to Ryan, wishing they brought another pair. "Is it?"

"Stanton . . ."

"What the hell is he doing here?"

"Obviously, he has something to do with People's First Delivery . . ." A pause. "And, why is he leaving by the alley?"

"Exactly my question! Anyone doing that usually doesn't want to be seen—especially someone of his stature."

Handing the binos back to her, Ryan pressed the ignition button, then buckled up. "Interesting he shows up within twenty-four hours of Dalca's execution . . ."

Colbie kept her eyes on Stanton as he climbed into a waiting black sedan. "Agreed." Another pause. "Time to get in touch with Jake . . ."

"You think there's a connection?"

A moment's silence. "I know there is . . ."

"I'm sorry I yelled . . ." Walker Newton apologized as he gently nuzzled Elaine's neck. "I just had a lot to do, and I was feeling the pressure." A slight nip.

"Ow! You know I don't like that—it reminds me of Eric!"

Another nuzzle. "Forgiven?"

Elaine turned, smiling. "Of course, silly—you know I can't stay mad at you."

With that, the two melded as one, each enjoying the company of the other, even if Walker were seeing her within the confines of duty.

A perk of sorts.

Knowing her husband wasn't due home until the following day, it was a situation Elaine could only dream of as she slipped out of Newton's bed shortly before midnight. Whether he were a light sleeper, she didn't know—it was, however, a chance she knew she must take.

Quietly, feet chilled against the slate floor, she padded to the living room, picked up her purse, then placed it by the massive front door. Then, her keys, carefully situated on top.

Once done, she returned to the bedroom, gathered her clothes, then headed for a small bathroom down the hall. Minutes later, she emerged, fully dressed, complete with a disposable rain poncho covering her from head to toe. Well, almost her toes—the tips of her shoes stuck out slightly.

Then, reaching into her designer skirt pocket, fingers wrapping around something cool yet unfamiliar, she withdrew her hand and aimed, firing two, silenced, well-placed rounds into her paramour's forehead.

How sad, she thought as she headed for the door, her back a little straighter than when she arrived that evening.

Such an unceremonious end . . .

CHAPTER 17

Jake shifted his cell to the other ear, then signaled to the hot dog vendor to keep the change. "I knew I'd seen him before—his name is Nash Hobbs."

"Hobbs? Are you sure?"

"Yeah—why? Do you know him?"

Colbie smiled. "Not really, but, I know of him. He's a private investigator, and a good one . . ."

"Then, what the hell is he doing with Constance?"

"Well, maybe they're acquaintances. I don't know about him, but she's been around Washington for a long time—it makes sense they'd know each other."

Jake was quiet, working through what he saw and what he felt when he saw Constance and Hobbs at the restaurant. "They looked pretty cozy . . ."

"Well, then, that's probably it! It's not a crime to be in a relationship last I heard . . ." Colbie laughed, hoping to quell his rising unease.

"No—it's something more. I feel it . . ."

Colbie glanced at Ryan who was pretending not to listen. For Jake to claim his abilities was a rarity, not to mention an ironclad indication he was on to something. "Okay—let's say there's something other than a personal relationship going on. What would that be?"

"I have no idea! But, look at it, Colbie—from the beginning, why did Harry Stanton need to speak to Derrick Dickson?" Without waiting for her answer, Jake ticked off chronological events since Colbie arrived in D.C. "Knowing Harry as I did, I wouldn't be surprised if he were into something no one knew anything about . . ."

"Except, maybe, a small circle of people . . ."

"Exactly—and, knowing Harry, it would be a group of people who stood to make a bunch of money."

"It also stands to reason his son would be part of it."

Switching his cell to the other ear, Jake leaned back in his chair. "That's what I think . . ."

After another ten, Colbie's cell faded to dead air as she tossed it on the couch. "That was interesting," she commented as Ryan closed his laptop.

"I gather something's up?"

"Well, maybe. Jake linked Constance Parnell . . ."

"Harry Stanton's assistant . . ."

"Correct. Anyway, Jake saw Constance and Nash Hobbs together at a restaurant, acting more than acquaintances."

"So?"

"That's what I thought—but, Jake seems to think there's more to it."

"Do you?"

Colbie shook her head, then leaned back on the couch, staring at the ceiling. "I don't know." A pause. "Maybe. I've known Jake for a long time, and my gut tells me to pay attention."

Ryan was quiet for a moment, thinking. "The same Hobbs in our line of business?"

A nod. "That's what has Jake curious—he feels it's more than coincidence Hobbs is with Harry's assistant."

"I can't say I blame him—it's a good bet Constance had her fingers in every political pie that concerned her boss."

"And, perhaps she has the same allegiance with Harry's son . . ."

"Maybe—at any rate, I decided not to tell him Eric Stanton paid a visit to People's First Delivery. If Stanton's being there is less than aboveboard, the less Jake knows, the better."

"From a political standpoint?"

"Precisely—as far as anyone knows, I'm a writer from his past. And, that's the way I want to keep it . . ."

By the end of the week, life in D.C. was back to normal, if there were such a thing, and Eric Stanton breezed in, surprising his wife with a bouquet of white roses. "For you, my dear!"

Of course, Elaine gushed, perhaps a little too much. But, knowing a different response could have bought her something she didn't want or need, it seemed a small price to pay. "They're lovely," she whispered, standing on her tiptoes to give him a light kiss. "I'll put them in water . . ."

He watched as she reached for a vase, then arranged each rose until it were just so. "Anything interesting happen while I was gone?"

She turned, smiling. "Interesting? Hardly! I have a few social engagements to plan for, but that's about it . . ." A pause as she cocked her head coyly. "There was one thing, though—someone in The Haven was found dead." Another pause. "Murder, they think . . ."

"The Haven? When?"

"A few nights ago—that's the last I heard on the news."

"But, murder? Did they say what happened?"

Elaine nodded. "Two bullets to the forehead, I think . . ."

As Stanton listened, a slight chill coursed his spine, accompanied by a sudden shudder. For some reason, his wife seemed—confident. Calculating.

Cold.

He said nothing, thinking of whom he knew in the ostentatious, gated community—such an exclusive enclave of pricey homes rarely received press for something so seemly. In the next thought, however, he figured it was none of his beeswax—whoever bought the farm didn't concern him.

Thank God . . .

By the end of the week, Colbie and Ryan packed their bags and headed for D.C., but only after a quick detour to Aspen. "Of course, I understand why we're going," Ryan commented as they waited for their commuter flight, "but, I just don't see the connection."

"Neither do I—that's the point." Colbie shot him a glance, somehow managing to squelch increasing irritation. "But, if Daria tells me to go somewhere, I'm going!"

"Okay! It was just a comment!"

Immediately, Colbie reached for his hand, giving it a squeeze. "I know—I'm sorry."

"Apology accepted—but, I don't get it. Something has you antsy, so care to share?" He grinned, knowing she hated that phrase.

A smile, then a gut laugh. "No! I don't care to share!"

And, that's how they left it—at least until dinner that night in a main street restaurant in Colorado's most exclusive ski town.

Colbie smiled at their server as she laid her menu on the table. "I'll have the prime rib with a salad," Colbie ordered. "No potato . . ."

Ryan glanced at her from over his menu. "No potato? Since when?"

"Since now! I have to drop a pound or two, if you must know!"

The server grinned as she topped off their wine, enjoying the playful banter, then headed to parts unknown. "What a nice young woman," Colbie commented. "I'm not sure I could do her job . . ."

"Agreed." A pause. "Did you notice?"

"Notice?"

"The hearing aids . . ."

Colbie was quiet, silently chastising herself for being blind to something that should've been obvious. "No," she finally answered. "I didn't . . ."

"Interesting, don't you think? I mean, we're here because of Daria, and she taught deaf students." He watched as Colbie took a sip of wine. "I don't know about you, but that's kind of like a two by four upside the head . . ."

"It could be coincidence . . ."

"Oh, please! You know damned well it isn't coincidence!"

"No, I don't know that—but, for the sake of spirited conversation, let's say it isn't. I'm not sure I feel comfortable pointing out her hearing issue . . ."

Ryan took a sip, glancing at a server passing their table. "Oh, I don't think you'll have too much trouble figuring out what to say . . ."

He was right.

By the time he slipped his credit card into the check folder, Colbie and their server were talking as if they were old friends. "Was it hard to get used to them," he heard her ask as she reached for her coat.

"Oh, no—if it weren't for Daria, though, I might not have tried them."

"Daria? A friend of yours?"

The server shook her head, smiling. "Not really—I happened to meet her the same way I'm talking to you." She paused, recalling the conversation.

"How interesting! When was that?"

"Maybe a year and a half ago—not long!" Another smile. "She noticed I was having trouble hearing, and she mentioned she taught at a school for the deaf in Europe."

"So, Daria encouraged you to get hearing aids?"

"Yes—but, what was really weird? A guy my dad works with has a daughter who's almost completely deaf, and I wound up waiting on him and his family not too long after I met Daria! She—his daughter—was in high school, I think."

Colbie sat back in her seat. "Seriously? Does she have hearing aids?"

The server nodded. "So, I figured if she could do it, I could, too!"

"Well, good for you! And, for what it's worth, you look fabulous! No one would ever know!" Colbie paused. "Do you ever hear from the daughter?"

"No—the only thing I remember is their last name. 'Dickson,' I think it was . . ."

Colbie glanced at Ryan, then focused again on their server. "Well, I'm sure she remembers you as much as you remember her," Colbie offered as she stood, signaling to Ryan it was time to go. "It's a small world, though, that's for sure!" A pause. "What does your dad do?"

"He's in politics . . ."

"Really? That must be interesting!" Colbie slipped on her gloves, then looked at Ryan. "Ready?"

Thanking their server for a delightful dinner, minutes later, both stood on the sidewalk, wet, spring snowflakes landing on their eyelashes. "Well, that was interesting," Ryan commented as they headed for their rental.

Suddenly, Colbie stopped, looking at her friend. "That's the connection . . ."

"Between . . ."

"Daria and the sign language—she was putting me in touch with the person who could give us what we needed!"

"Or, who. . ."

"Yep!" Colbie started for the corner, looking both ways before crossing even though there was little traffic. "Derrick Dickson . . ."

CHAPTER 18

*E*laine nodded silently as she served canapés to each, then quietly left the room, closing the door gently behind her. Quickly, she headed for the kitchen and into the massive pantry, flicking off the light, just in case anyone came looking.

As carefully as possible, she moved the oatmeal, snatching her cell from its hiding place, then tapping it to life, accessing a newly installed app guaranteed to tell her everything she needed to know.

Clandestine surveillance?

She couldn't call it anything else.

After all, she learned from the best.

The tricky part was taking the risk to have the necessary equipment professionally installed—if anyone of importance caught wind of her duplicity?

A storm would certainly rage.

If not? Well, let's just say an advantageous position is the envy of all politicians—and, their wives.

So, there Elaine Stanton stood—in a dark pantry surrounded by ingredients representing the sum of her talents, eavesdropping on conversations not meant for anyone's ears except the speaker's colleagues.

"This obviously presents a problem . . ." Laced with irritation and disagreeable disdain, Nash Hobbs's voice reminded Elaine of a high-pitched whine she heard when her granddaddy's tractor nearly blew up on the Virginia family farm thirty-five years prior.

"Obviously, that's why we're here . . ." Her husband matched Hobbs's irritation with his own, coupled with a prolonged, accusatory glance at each person in the room. "How much damage can Walker Newton do from the morgue?"

Taking a protracted puff on his cigar, Hobbs placed the smoldering stub in the ashtray. "Plenty." Then, he turned his attention to Stanton. "How was your trip to Vegas, Eric?"

"My trip?" Stanton lit a cigar of his own, then reached for his cocktail as he tried to figure out how Hobbs knew. "Uneventful . . ."

"You went to Vegas?" Constance's shrill voice was an unwelcome interruption, prompting Eric to shoot her a disapproving glare.

"Yes—I had family business to attend to." A weighted pause. "Why are you so interested?"

As Elaine listened, there was no question it was a marvelous performance, her husband's adroit maneuvering an ability learned from his father. Rarely, however, did anyone choose to confront it for what it truly was . . .

Bullshit.

"As I see it, Mr. Arlington, we have a few things to discuss—and, I appreciate your meeting with me on such short notice." Colbie smiled, making little progress as she tried to tune in—if Frank Arlington were anything, it was cold, bordering on unfriendly.

"Yes—I suppose we do." He rose, closed the conference room door, then again took his seat across from her. "You first, Ms. Colleen . . ."

First to ask questions was a position Colbie particularly enjoyed. Picking for vital information from an unwilling participant usually proved tedious, the results tenuous, and it was clear she was growing weary of her investigative chase. "I know you're a busy man," she began, not taking her eyes from him, "so, I'll be as succinct as possible." A dramatic pause. "What was Eric Stanton doing at People's First Delivery in Vegas a few days ago?"

Usually, in an investigative interview, it takes a few minutes to get warmed up, at least enough so to anticipate and gauge one's academic or personal response. Colbie, however, was ready to shoot from both barrels. "On Tuesday, I believe . . ."

There also comes a time in such an interrogation when it's clear someone is lying. "Why would I know what Eric Stanton is doing? He's nothing to me . . ."

Fib number one.

"Perhaps, Mr. Arlington, it would be good for you to recall why I enjoy the reputation I have for solving investigations."

"I don't know what you mean . . ."

"Oh, of course, you do—so, if you want me to continue on this case, I suggest you stop lying. You know damned well why Eric Stanton was in Vegas . . ." A pause. "Did you send him?"

A wry smile. "Send him? As in to 'do our bidding?'" Arlington hesitated, a slight smile playing on his lips. "I'm afraid you're barking up the wrong tree, Ms. Colleen."

"Then, why don't you set me straight?"

Silence.

"Fine, Mr. Arlington—your message is loud and clear." Colbie stood, then headed for the door. "You'll have my invoice by the close of today's business . . ."

"Sit down, Ms. Colleen! Drama doesn't become you . . ."

"I beg your pardon?" Colbie launched the political executive a glare usually saved for the most serious, disrespectful infractions.

"Please, Ms. Colleen—sit down. You're correct—we have much to discuss."

In that moment, Colbie realized defeat and resignation were two things to which Frank Arlington was unaccustomed. "Are you suggesting we begin again," she asked with a smile as she took her seat at the conference table.

"Yes—and, please accept my apology. It's been a long, interesting week . . ."

So, hatchets buried, Frank Arlington confided everything to the investigator who refused to let go, much like a dog with a bone. By the time Colbie walked out of Arlington's front door, a spring chill claimed the late afternoon air, little of her initial hypothesis remaining. As she walked to her rental, however?

A new one took its place.

Right on time, Elaine knocked gently before entering, sweeping the room with a professional eye. "More canapés?" A smile. "I can't let you be with an empty plate, now, can I?"

"Thank you, Elaine—these are absolutely scrumptious!" Constance reached for two more, carefully placing them on her plate.

Eric, it seemed, wasn't quite so delighted with his wife's impromptu appearance, a stabbing glare indicative of his displeasure. "Thank you, darling. I'll ring you when we need something . . ."

"Perfect!" Again, she smiled at everyone, Nash Hobbs not quite so enamored with their hostess. If there were one thing he knew?

The look of eyes not missing a thing.

"So, what do we do now?" Eric recaptured his guests' attention, his tone somewhat accusatory as his wife closed the door. "Bucur can't handle anything without Dalca . . ."

Silent agreement.

"And," Stanton continued, "with Newton pushing up daisies, it's safe to say we just relinquished control."

Constance stuffed a canapé in her mouth, then patted her lips with a delicate napkin. "That's not all we have to worry about, gentlemen . . ."

All eyes turned to her, waiting for another shoe to drop.

"What about Dickson," she asked, knowing full well if they didn't take care of the senator's duplicity, trouble would come knockin'. After all, he was the main reason they were meeting without him—with Newton gone, however, a reasonable solution quickly became out of reach.

But, Constance wasn't done. "And, Powers? He's been sticking his nose where it doesn't belong . . ."

Eric eyed his father's former assistant. "How do you know?"

"Because I've had him under surveillance for months." A brief second while she polished off the last canapé. "Not only at his home, but within the Capitol's walls, as well . . ."

Another lip pat. "Luckily, my former colleagues don't mind sharing a little political gossip every now and then . . ."

"Get to the point, Constance! What does Powers have to do with any of this?"

His was precisely the arrogance and dictatorial attitude Constance hated—not only about him, but his father as well.

You see, Constance Parnell wasn't exactly who she was cracked up to be, and rarely a moment went by when she wasn't thinking about exacting revenge. And, why not? The abuse Harry Stanton heaped on her during their working years was enough to last her a lifetime. So, when she had the opportunity for payback when Eric Stanton came calling . . .

How could she refuse?

One thing about a professional hit—no fuss, no mess, no leaving a trail. Homicide detectives had a few suspects, of course, but nothing they could really sink their teeth into. All they knew?

Someone wanted Costin Dalca dead.

They weren't, however, about to give up that easily, so when they decided to pay People's First Delivery a visit for the third time, it was clear the young receptionist was more than rattled. "I told you," she whined, "the last time I saw Mr. Dalca was when he called me into his office to look at the security footage from the day before!"

Detective Daniken glanced at his partner, then scanned the building's outer office. "She didn't tell us that, did she, Scanlan?"

"No, sir—not once."

"That's what I thought . . ." It was a moment when the good detective had to decide upon his position—make the twenty-something bubble head feel guilt ridden, or get down to the reason they were there. "Okay—I'm sure it was an oversight on your part." A pause. "What was on the tape?"

"And, why did he call you in to look at it," Detective Scanlan asked.

Jessica turned to the junior detective. "Because he wanted to know about two people on the surveillance footage."

"Who?"

"Mr. and Mrs. Blickenstaff . . ."

"What did they want?"

"He wanted to know how quickly we could move him to Phoenix."

"What about her?"

"I don't know—she wandered around outside, saying she'd meet him in the car."

Daniken was quiet for a moment, thinking. "I'll need that tape," he finally ordered.

Without hesitation, the young woman retrieved the tape from the safe, handing it to him. "Do you think they killed Mr. Dalca," she asked, her wide-eyed innocence rather refreshing.

But, neither Daniken nor Scanlan answered. With a silent nod, they left, tape in hand, leaving a woman who undoubtedly knew too much to wonder . . .

Do they suspect me?

CHAPTER 19

Elaine stepped aside, opening the stately front door. "Eric isn't here, I'm afraid." In years past, her role when greeting guests would've been more like that of a servant. That day?

Newfound confidence was in full swing.

Detective Decklin Kilgarry smiled, lending a particular sweetness to his overall good looks. "We'll only be a minute— I'm sure we can get all the information we need from you, if you have time."

"Well . . ."

Another drop-dead smile. "Like I said, we'll be out of your hair in ten minutes. We're talking to everyone in the neighborhood . . ."

"Well, I guess I have time—but, only ten minutes. I was just getting ready to leave . . ."

The detective glanced at her purse on the table by the front door, car keys placed carefully on top. "I promise . . ." Another smile, accompanied by the 'Scouts' honor' sign.

How could she say no? "Please—come in."

Within seconds, she gestured to two formal chairs in the sitting room, seating herself directly across from them on a pricey love seat. "I assume this is about the death of that poor man from The Haven . . ."

"You knew him?"

Elaine blushed. "Good heavens, no! But, why else would you be here?"

Kilgarry eyed the fragile woman, his gut telling him to pay attention. "Well, as it happens, you're right—Detective Marsh and I are speaking to those who may have seen something."

"You think I saw something?"

"Did you?"

Then, without so much as a blink, a side of the woman no one knew, took charge. "I rarely go anywhere, Detective. And, if I noticed anything, I certainly would've been the first to contact you . . ." She paused, wondering if the detectives knew who she was. "My husband, Eric Stanton, will be home shortly—I'm certain he'll tell you the same thing."

In Elaine's mind?

A little namedropping never hurt.

"Stanton?" Detective Kilgarry's eyebrows arched with insincere astonishment. "The politician?" He glanced at his partner, then focused again on Elaine.

"Yes—I'm sure you know him."

"Of him—we've heard his name." He hesitated, quickly reassessing how to conduct his questioning. With the clout of one of Washington's most revered families in his crosshairs, it was wise to tread softly.

"Well, as I said, he'll tell you the same thing." She stood. "Now, I'm afraid I must go . . ."

Although Kilgarry hated leaving questioning to a later date, there was little doubt he had some thinking to do. Of all the people he questioned that day, no one—other than Elaine Stanton—piqued his interest. "I understand—and, I'll take you up on your offer to speak to your husband at another time."

With that, the two detectives headed for the next house, neither saying a word until they were well out of sight. "Well, what do you think?" Detective Marsh glanced at his partner, then kept his eyes on the road.

"I'm not sure . . ."

"Harry Stanton's kid?" A moment's silence. "I hope to God he doesn't have anything to do with it—what a freakin' hornet's nest!"

Pulling into the customary circular drive lined with flowering spring shrubs a quarter mile from the Stantons, Decklin Kilgarry unhitched his seatbelt and patted his sports jacket inside pocket, making sure his small notepad was there. Then, he focused on his partner. "Know what I think?"

"I can guess . . ."

"Elaine Stanton knows something . . ."

"So, that's it—Derrick Dickson is a member of the Arlington Group, and his cover is blown."

Ryan was quiet as he tried to make sense of Colbie's side of the conversation. "Cover for what?"

"Infiltrating Eric Stanton's inner circle . . ."

"Okay—and, why was Dickson a mole?"

Colbie typed a few notes on her laptop before answering, making sure she kept the salient points of her conversation with Frank Arlington fresh in her mind. "Because there's suspicion of a certain group of politicians involved in what's going on at People's First Delivery . . ."

"Which is?"

"That's just it—Arlington isn't sure, and that's why Dickson was inserted into the group."

"And, I'm guessing that's why Arlington called you in the first place . . ."

Colbie nodded. "Exactly."

"Then, why didn't he tell you everything from the git?"

"Who knows? Maybe he was hoping I'd learn something they could use right away, and I'd be gone. You know—done deal."

"I guess . . ."

"After talking with Arlington, the one thing I'm sure about is my connection with Daria was meant to lead us to Dickson. And, it makes sense—he's the pivotal point."

"Meaning?"

"Remember when Harry Stanton and Dickson had that conversation, and Jake saw them talking at the Capitol?"

"Yes, but that doesn't mean anything. Jake didn't hear them, so he has no idea what they were talking about . . ."

"True, but I've known him for a long time and, when he senses something, it's usually true."

"Still . . ."

Colbie shot him a glance. "If you remember, it was Jake who suspected something was up—maybe not for you, but it's good enough for me!"

Ryan stood, grabbed his laptop, then headed for the door. "Fine! When you're ready to listen to another opinion, let me know!"

Seconds later, he was gone, leaving Colbie to cope with a quickly seething anger. If she were to be honest, since working with Ryan again, all it served to do was solidify her decision to leave their investigative firm. After being by herself for so long after Brian's passing—although, liking her alone time came as a bit of surprise—she had no intention of giving it up. As far as returning to her former life?

Decision made.

"We had visitors today . . ."

Eric Stanton didn't bother to look at his wife as he sat staring at his laptop, checking the daily stocks.

"Did you hear me, Eric?"

"I heard you—we had visitors today."

Elaine struggled to keep tears from welling. There was only so much a person could endure, and she was, without doubt, at the end of her patience with her loving husband. "Do you want to know who?"

"Okay—who?"

She smiled slightly, knowing her next revelation would certainly snap him to attention. "A very nice Detective Kilgarry, and his partner—I don't recall his name."

Stanton glanced at her, then sat back in his desk chair, allowing her a fraction of his attention. "What did they want?"

"They were questioning everyone in the neighborhood about that poor man who was murdered in the Haven. Samantha Eversol called me as soon as they left her place, so I was expecting them—but, I told them I had to leave ."

"Okay—so? We didn't have anything to do with it, so it's no concern of mine." With a soft snort, he returned to his work, obviously not understanding one thing . . .

He should've been concerned.

It wasn't until a full four weeks later word circulated about the particular's of Walker Newton's unfortunate demise. Two well-placed rounds to the forehead could've been done by anyone, really, and, by the time Detective Kilgarry returned to speak to Eric Stanton? Well, let's just say a month's time provided the slippery snake of a politician enough time to plan.

The same for the D.C. detective.

"I'm sure I have nothing of interest for you, Detective— of course, it's never pleasant when someone from our adjacent neighborhood falls prey to such a thing, but, the truth is all I know is what's on the news. Nothing else . . ."

"I appreciate that, but, if you don't mind, I'll need to ask only a couple of questions . . ."

Stanton nodded. "I understand . . ."

"My research into Mr. Newton's past was particularly interesting, given his time spent around the Capitol—several of your colleagues recalled seeing him, although most had no idea of his name."

"My colleagues?"

"Well, yes—when I learned of Mr. Newton's profession, it made sense to find out as much as possible." A pause. "You know—follow the lead. I'm sure you'll agree . . ."

"Of course—but, I'm not sure what you mean. Mr. Newton's profession?"

"Yes—well, it came to my attention over the past few weeks that Mr. Newton was quite an accomplished private investigator."

Eric said nothing, his stomach beginning to churn with realization.

"And," Detective Kilgarry continued, "it seems he did quite a bit of work for a few of your associates."

"Well, that may be, but, I assure you he didn't work for me . . ."

Elaine stood on the other side of the door to the library, her ear pressed against the cool wood—disappointed, the sound of muffled voices was all she could hear. It was then she realized—obviously, her husband was lying as any good Stanton would do. The only problem with that was she knew the truth . . .

A fact that could come back to bite him, if he didn't mind his Ps and Qs.

Nash Hobbs placed his cigar in the ashtray gifted to him by his cousin, intuition telling him walls were beginning to close. There was a reason he was so good at this job and, when his gut kicked in, it was always cause for concern—but, it wasn't until Kilgarry and Marsh knocked on his residence door did he know it was time to jump ship.

Although he chose not to mention it to his inner circle, including Constance, there was no doubt Newton was about to be fingered for eighty-sixing Costin Dalca. After weeks of investigation, one clue led to another, and it wasn't long until Vegas's finest put two and two together. In his mind?

The connecting thread was beginning to fray.

Of course, he had nothing to do with Newton's murder and, if the media were to be trusted, no one he knew was on the authorities' short list.

That, too, was cause for concern.

"How can I help you, Detective?"

Kilgarry clicked his pen, pad poised for interesting notes. "I appreciate your making the time . . ." A second pen click. "How well did you know Walker Newton?"

A moment to think. "Well, as you can imagine, Detective, those in our profession have a tendency to make enemies—although, that's never our intention."

"What profession is that, Mr. Hobbs?"

Hobbs smiled, amused by the detective's insipid question. "Please, Detective—let's not do the dance. You know exactly what I do for a living—and, I'm proud to say I'm very good at it."

"Even so, Mr. Hobbs, I'll appreciate your answering my question."

A slight weight shift. "I'm a seasoned private investigator, Detective. A private investigator for twenty-five years . . ."

Kilgarry smiled. "That's a hell of an accomplishment in any profession!"

"Indeed."

"So, I repeat—how well did you know Walker Newton?"

"As a colleague, I knew his work because I hired him to do the legwork I can no longer handle. His personal life is another story . . ."

Of course, that was a bald-faced lie—Nash Hobbs knew damned well Newton spent free time with Elaine Stanton. There was something about her he didn't trust, so it seemed the perfect ploy for Newton to keep company with the woman most considered battered and bruised.

Mentally and physically.

"Why was Newton in Las Vegas, Mr. Hobbs?"

"I have no idea—since he wasn't there working a case for me, I can only assume he was there on his own. You know—personal time."

"Do you know Costin Dalca?"

"No."

Kilgarry was quiet for a moment, considering his next move. There was a lot to be said for subterfuge, but, in the long run, honesty seemed the best approach. "That's interesting, Mr. Hobbs, because there seems to be a direct link to you . . ."

"That's impossible! What on earth could I possibly have to do with . . ." Then, he stopped, recognizing the detective's technique. "There is no link to me, Detective . . ."

"Really? I'm afraid I know otherwise, Mr. Hobbs."

It was then Nash Hobbs stood. "I'll be contacting my attorney, Detective Kilgarry . . ."

CHAPTER 20

After harsh words the previous evening, it seemed best to leave Ryan to his own thoughts for the day—and, it was better for Colbie, as well. Although she hated when they argued, she could no longer falsely convince herself returning to their partnership was the right thing to do. *Too much water under the bridge,* she thought as she climbed into her rental, *and I don't want to ruin our friendship.*

As she sat, regret and sorrow singed her heart . . .

It was time.

To most, Elaine Stanton was little more than a puppet for her husband's desires—although, few would exhibit the poor taste to ever breathe such words to anyone outside the protective confines of their own bedrooms. Such conversations were often reserved for pillow talk, everyone knowing she endured what no woman should, and it was with a sense of sadness those on the periphery chose to say nothing.

Realizations not lost on the politician's wife.

Even so, she held her head high, refusing to succumb to paltry gossip—doing otherwise wouldn't honor the revered Stanton name. Besides, it was risky not to play the part to which her husband was accustomed—it was also prudent to protect herself at any cost. The result?

A lonely existence.

So, when Walker Newton paid her more than a little attention, it was something she found enjoyable, despite the considerable risks—and, there were risks.

"I'm sorry to bother you again, Mrs. Stanton—but, I'm wondering if I might have a few moments of your time." Decklin Kilgarry flashed the smile she dreamed of on more than one occasion.

"Of course! Please come in . . ."

As it turned out, the dutiful Elaine followed her husband's orders quite well. Certain her performance would be to his expectations, she invited her guests to sit, offering tea and a treat she baked that morning.

Declined.

"Now, what can I do for you, Detective?"

Without looking at her, Kilgarry reviewed his previous notes. "Well, I have a few more questions—the last time I was here, I felt as if we left things . . . unfinished."

Elaine said nothing for a moment, quickly recalling their conversation. "Well, I don't know what that could be—I told you everything I know. I didn't know . . ."

"Walker Newton."

"Yes—I didn't know him, so I'm afraid I can't tell you any more than last time."

"Are you familiar with the name Costin Dalca, Mrs. Stanton?"

Finally—a question she could answer without lying. "No, I don't think so . . ."

"Your husband hasn't mentioned it?"

A narrowing stare. "No."

"Have you ever been to Las Vegas?"

"Well, of course! Who hasn't?" It was then Elaine realized the detective's questions were leading her in an uncomfortable direction. "Really, Detective—if you're going to ask me about my husband, I'm afraid I must decline."

"Why is that?"

"Because I know nothing!"

Decklin looked up from his notes. "Well, you see, I find that a bit puzzling . . ."

Silence.

Of course, Kilgarry's questions were based on absolutely nothing—no evidence, gossip, or anything else causing him to look at Harry Stanton's daughter-in-law with a jaded eye. But, what he did know?

Elaine Stanton was lying through her teeth.

Again, Detective Kilgarry looked at his notes, but only for show. "Let's get back to Walker Newton, Mrs. Stanton. Are you familiar with Nash Hobbs?"

"Nash Hobbs? Well . . . no."

"You've heard the name?"

"It sounds familiar . . ."

"You either have, or you haven't."

Elaine stood. "I find your tone insulting, Detective. I don't recall the names of my husband's colleagues . . ."

The detective stayed seated. "Please sit down, Mrs. Stanton. All I'm trying to do is figure out who decided to end Walker Newton's life . . . nothing more."

But, Detective Kilgarry got what he needed. Although he wanted to press, experience told him another time would be better.

He stood. "Thank you," he offered, motioning to Marsh. "We'll let ourselves out . . ."

Minutes later, the two detectives pulled out of the Stanton driveway, both silent just in case. "What was that bullshit about Vegas," Marsh finally asked, pulling into traffic.

"Maybe nothing . . ."

"Then, why?"

"Before we left the precinct, I got an interesting call from Detective Daniken, asking about Walker Newton . . ."

"Who's he?"

"A Vegas detective I've known for years . . ."

"So, what about Newton?"

"It seems there's evidence regarding a murder."

Marsh glanced at his boss, trying to fit the pieces together. "Costin Dalca?"

Kilgarry nodded. "Yep. I don't know how things are going to come together, but my gut tells me the Stanton name is involved . . ."

"So, to what do I owe the pleasure?" Jake Powers grinned, then placed his dinner menu to the side.

Colbie smiled, then took a sip of wine. "I'm tying up loose ends . . ."

"You mean you're ending the case—although, I'm still not sure what your 'case' is!"

Another smile. "No—I mean I'm tying together what we know . . . we have too many things that don't fit a specific narrative, but I know they're leading to the same place—or, thing."

"So, what can I do?"

Suddenly, Colbie reached into her messenger bag, extracting a photograph. "Do you recognize him?"

Jake stared at it for a moment, then sat back in his chair. "That's the guy I saw in Seattle—you know, when you and I met at the restaurant. Who is he?"

"Walker Newton."

"Who the hell is Walker Newton?"

"A private investigator—whose boss's name is Nash Hobbs."

Jake was quiet, his mind racing as he thought of his recent suspicions. "Was he tailing me?"

Colbie shook her head, then placed her wine goblet on the table. "I don't know—but, if he were, he won't be anymore. He's dead . . ."

"What?"

Another nod. "Yep—two shots to the forehead."

"A hit?"

"It seems so—or, made to look like one."

It was then Colbie had to decide—clue Jake in about her conversation with Frank Arlington, or keep things to herself.

Jake noticed. "You know you can trust me . . ."

"I know." An uncertain pause. "Have you ever heard of Frank Arlington?"

"Of course—he heads up a watchdog group, but I don't know him personally." He hesitated, wondering why a big name such as Arlington's was coming into their conversation. "Why? Is he involved with your investigation?"

Colbie nodded slightly, took another sip of wine, then focused again on her friend. "As I said, I'm not sure how things are coming together—so, I can use your help."

"What about your partner?"

A topic Colbie didn't care to discuss. "He's working on other things . . ."

Hers was a tone Jake recognized, indicating it wasn't the time nor place to be inquisitive. "Okay—shoot. I'll tell you what I know . . ."

So, for the next hour Colbie brought her childhood friend up to speed, leaving nothing untouched. "The names at the top of our list are Eric Stanton—because we saw him in the alley next to People's First Delivery—Nash Hobbs, and Walker Newton.

"Don't forget Constance Parnell . . ."

"Yes, but I don't think she has a significant role in anything. She may have been around Washington for years, but her capacity is greatly diminished when it comes to clout."

"Maybe—I wouldn't count on it, though. If she's involved with Eric Stanton? I'd be willing to bet there's something to it other than money . . ."

"I don't follow . . ."

"Well, it's no secret Constance wasn't exactly the queen of the ball at the Capitol—more often than not, her personality was sour, bitter, and downright unpleasant."

"Seriously? I didn't get that impression, at all."

Jake laughed, enjoying the stunned look on her face. "It's Washington, Colbie—nothing is as it seems. Lying is a way of life—and, I bet if you asked anyone, they'd tell you the same thing about Constance." He hesitated, but only for a moment. "Everyone has an agenda . . ."

"I know—you're right. I tend to believe the best about people . . ."

"You always have."

A comfortable silence.

Finally, Colbie tackled the reason she was in D.C. "And, that brings me to one more person on our radar—perhaps, the most important."

"And, that is?"

"Derrick Dickson . . ."

By the time Colbie made it back to the hotel, blossoming resolve dug in. Relegating her feelings about Ryan and their investigative firm to the backseat, she popped him a text, suggesting they meet in her room to discuss her dinner with Jake. "I decided we needed to bring him up to speed about everything—we have to start tying things together."

Ryan grinned, knowing harsh words were behind them. "Agreed. What did he say?"

"Well, not much, except for Constance Parnell . . ."

"What about her?"

Colbie took a drink of water, thinking about what Jake told her. "Apparently, everyone who had anything to do with her hated her guts . . ."

"Everyone, except Harry."

"True—but, that also tells me a lot about Senator Harry Stanton. He had to count on Constance for everything, and it makes me wonder if Eric does the same thing . . ."

"Unfortunately, we'll probably never know—but, how about if I do a little friendly surveillance on Ms. Constance Parnell?"

"Exactly what I was thinking—we know she was at the Stanton home when we surveilled it, although, at the time, we didn't know it was her. Or, anyone else for that matter . . ."

"Well, now we know—or, at least, suspect—there's an allegiance of some sort between Stanton, Hobbs, Newton, Constance . . ." Ryan's voice trailed, thinking of who he missed.

"Don't forget Stanton's wife—she's not off my radar yet."

"Nor mine . . ."

Derrick Dickson glanced at his wife, unclear if she heard him correctly. "What do you mean," she asked. "You're telling us we need to leave?"

"Only for a little while—I don't want anything happening to you and Harper."

"For God's sake, Derrick! What the hell is going on?"

As much as he didn't want to tell her, it was time for the truth. "A lot . . ."

Both sat at the kitchen table, Dickson's wife twisting an unused napkin in her hand. As you can imagine, no wife wants to hear that—but, after her husband stopped talking, her eyes filled with tears. "What's going to happen to you?"

"Good question, but I don't want you and Harper in the thick of it. And, you can't go to your mother's . . ."

"Then, where?"

Pained silence descended, both carrying unfamiliar uncertainty. "I'll think of something," he told her as he stood, pulled her to him, then kissed the top of her head.

"What about Harper? School?"

"She'll have to do her schooling from home for a while."

"Oh Derrick! She's going to hate that!"

Again, he kissed the top of his wife's head, feeling her anguish as he wrapped her tighter. "We're all going to hate it—at least for a while."

And, that's how they left it, fresh fear positioning to guide their days. All they knew?

Things were about to change.

CHAPTER 21

*I*ntelligence is one of those things measured not only by thought, but by resulting actions, as well—at least, that seems the best approach when attempting to ascertain one's merits. Unfortunately, such a scientific approach isn't interesting to many—they prefer to believe what they see with their own eyes. So, when Nash Hobbs decided to meet clandestinely with Eric Stanton, he knew it could be one of the dumbest things he ever did.

"One of D.C.'s finest paid me a visit," Hobbs informed his employer and colleague, then waited for the reaction he most expected. "I thought you should know . . ."

Exactly what Eric Stanton didn't want to hear.

It didn't take a genius to figure out Decklin Kilgarry was making the rounds to those within Stanton's circle, and he wasn't going to put up with it for one second. "What did he want?"

"He asked about Newton."

Brief silence.

"After that, he asked about Costin Dalca . . ."

As the private investigator's words hit their mark, it was the first time in Eric Stanton's life he felt . . . well, alone. No longer was his father waiting in the wings to correct his son's innumerable wrongs, leaving anyone with a brain to realize the politician was starting to break a sweat.

"Did you hear me, Eric? I said Kilgarry asked about Dalca . . ."

The explosion Hobbs expected was simmering, yet never releasing—unimaginable to the seasoned private investigator. Even so, strange things happen when realization rears its ugly head—you know, the moment when the house of cards so carefully and painstakingly built shudders for the first time.

"I heard you."

Hobbs stared at Stanton, wondering if Harry's mini-me finally lost his marbles. Still, he said nothing, waiting.

"What do you suggest," Eric finally asked.

"The first thing is none of us meet after I walk out of your door. Both of us know Kilgarry has his hounds on us . . ."

Stanton nodded. "This changes everything. If we don't get out of this, we're done . . ."

Within the week, Derrick Dickson's goodbyes to his family were in the books, allowing him to turn his attention to what he knew he had to do. Ever since he landed in Washington so many years prior, never did he think he'd be in such a position. But, when he realized countless lives were at stake?

Decision made.

A quick Internet search provided the number and, within a few seconds, he connected. Moments later, it was too late to reconsider. "Detective Kilgarry?"

Back in Vegas, Colbie and Ryan checked the map, again in unfamiliar territory as they tackled additional research on People's First Delivery. "At least this time, we have more to go on—and, the first thing I want to do is have a chat with the detective who's spearheading the investigation."

"Daniken, I believe . . ."

She nodded. "That's right—he can save us a lot of time."

"That's if he's willing to talk . . ."

"True—but, I think he will, especially when he realizes there's a connection to our case."

"Which is?"

For a second, Colbie said nothing, realizing it was the first time she had to actually define their investigation. "Well, right now, it's all about finding out what Eric Stanton has to do with Costin Dalca . . ."

"His murder?"

Another nod. "That, and whether Dalca had contact with anyone else in Washington . . ."

Ryan eyed her, a sense of unease beginning to rise. "What makes you think that?"

"Because, when you really think about it, all of our players are members of a very small circle—and, at first glance, they don't seem to go together.

"Such as Constance Parnell's being in the thick of it?"

"Exactly."

Both were quiet until Colbie stood and grabbed her jacket. "Let's go . . ."

Ryan snatched the map, then his coat. "Where to?"

"First, I want to get eyes on where Dalca lived—after that, we're going to pay a surprise visit to Jessica."

"At People's First?"

"Yep." A pause. "Will you please grab the map?" Colbie rifled through her bag for her sunglasses, then held the door for her partner. "After you . . ."

"I'm not going to lie, Senator—your call came as quite a surprise." Decklin Kilgarry smiled as he took a seat across from Derrick Dickson in his comfortable den.

"I'm sure it did, Detective—and, I appreciate your willingness to meet me on my own turf, so to speak." A pause. "What I have to tell you may take a while, and I want you to be as comfortable as possible . . ." A smile played on Dickson's lips, indicating the subtle sarcasm.

"Much appreciated," Kilgarry commented as he plucked the ubiquitous notepad from his shirt pocket. "Now—why am I here?"

"Before we begin, may I get you a bottled water? You're probably going to need it . . ." With that, Dickson crossed to a small refrigerator built into strong, teakwood bookcases. "I'd offer you something stronger, but . . . you know." He smiled, returning with the water, its cap loosened. "Careful—I twisted the top."

Heeding the warning, Detective Kilgarry carefully placed the water on an artisan-made coaster. "I'll say one thing for ya—you know how to pique curiosity!"

"As it should be . . ." Then, Derrick sat and took a deep breath, squaring his attention on the D.C. detective. "I suppose it'll be helpful if I start at the beginning . . ."

Usually and at just the right time, opportunity for reassessment presents itself—unwanted, perhaps, but seldom does that seem to matter. It arrives anyway, caring little about possible repercussions—kind of like the Grim Reaper showing up unexpectedly at the front door.

And, that's where Constance Parnell was in her life—reassessing. During past weeks, life with Nash Hobbs wasn't as pleasant as it first was, sparking doubt whether he was, in fact, the man for her.

But, that wasn't all.

The more Harry Stanton played in her mind, the more disdain and contempt she felt for his son. How much longer she could carry on her charade, she didn't know—all she knew was exacting long-awaited revenge was on the horizon. What did that mean for playing her cards?

Keep the ace.

Naturally, there were considerations—should she decide the time were ripe for sending the arrogant Eric Stanton up the river, necessity dictated doing so in an undisclosed location with the promise of immunity—otherwise, her lips were sealed.

So, what was her tipping point?

Nash Hobbs's not kicking Decklin Kilgarry to the curb when he first graced Hobbs's doorstep.

In her mind, Kilgarry should've remained on the other side of the door, her better half insisting on an attorney immediately.

The whole thing caused such a rift between them, she hadn't seen Hobbs in nearly three weeks, their separation fraught with implication. *Maybe it's time*, Constance thought as she exacted a plan, making certain to write nothing down.

Maybe it's time . . .

"Thank you for taking time out of your day to see me," Colbie commented, shaking Detective Daniken's hand. "Much appreciated . . ."

The Vegas detective smiled, gesturing to an old school, hard-backed chair in front of his desk. "I'm afraid it's not too comfortable," he commented. "But, it serves the purpose . . ."

"After a late-night flight, I'm pretty sure anything will be comfortable right now!" Colbie returned his smile as she sat, then placed her messenger bag on the floor next to her.

Daniken sat back in his chair, eyeing her intently. "So, what can I do for you? I believe you said it's about Costin Dalca's murder?" When Colbie contacted him, he had little time to do a quick Internet search, so he knew nothing of her, the investigation firm, or her success. "And, why should I talk to you?"

"Ah! The direct approach," Colbie laughed. "I like it!"

So, for the next several minutes, she offered a quick, verbal bio and recap. "And, that's why I'm here—after I heard about Costin Dalca's murder and witnessed Eric Stanton climbing into a black sedan in the alley beside People's First Delivery, it was clear there was a connection between Dalca and him. What, I'm not sure . . ."

As Daniken listened, it was obvious Colbie Colleen could be an asset to his investigation. "What do you know about Eric Stanton," he asked, hoping she would be aboveboard.

She wasn't.

"The question is what do you know about him?"

The detective said nothing for a few moments, thinking. Finally, he answered. "I know he's in politics . . ."

A nod. "Yes—his father was Harry Stanton."

"I'm afraid I'm not the most political guy on the planet—what should I know about both?"

"Harry Stanton was a fifty-year politico who dropped dead recently and unexpectedly, leaving his son to carry the Stanton torch." A pause. "When I first got involved with this case . . ."

"Which case is that, Ms. Colleen?"

It was the second time she was asked that question, and answering wasn't any easier. So, Colbie began at the beginning, telling Daniken about Jake Powers's contacting her because he felt something was wrong. "I say 'felt,' Detective, because I'm what most people call an 'intuitive.' Jake is one, as well, and I trust his instincts." Another pause as she tried to determine the detective's response.

Nothing.

"So, I headed to Washington—and, that's when things started to take shape, though not quickly." As Colbie explained her involvement in the case, as much as she wanted to tell the detective about Daria, she knew it wouldn't be well-received. Sitting across from him, his energy was strong. Willful. Determined.

"Then, almost as an adjunct to my reason for being in Washington, my current client contacted me about coming to Vegas to check out People's First Delivery . . ."

For the first time during their conversation, Detective Scott Daniken showed a flicker of special interest. "When was that again," he asked, scooting forward in his chair.

"Three weeks ago."

"Why is your client interested in People's First Delivery?"

"Well, until recently, I wasn't too sure—one thing I was certain about, however, was they weren't telling me the whole story." Before Colbie called the detective, she decided if she were going to contact him regarding one of his cases, he deserved to know everything, including cluing him in on the Arlington Group.

"Do you know it now?"

"The whole story?" Colbie nodded. "Yes—and, it's more than disturbing."

It was then Detective Scott Daniken knew hers was a story he needed to know. "I have time . . ."

CHAPTER 22

*D*errick Dickson again crossed to the small bar, poured a scotch, neat, then returned to his chair. "To calm my nerves," he laughed, making himself comfortable.

"Whatever works . . ."

"So, where to begin?" A pause. "How about the last five years . . ."

"Again, I'm here to listen . . ."

"I know." Another pause. "When I decided to enter politics, Detective, it wasn't for the glory or power coming with it. No, for some reason, I thought I could actually do some good . . ."

"A laudable intent . . ."

"Perhaps—but, it wasn't long before I was inducted into the seamier side of political life. I fell for it, too—I mean, who wouldn't enjoy perks of which many only dare to dream?" Although he wasn't expecting an answer to his question, Dickson paused anyway, perhaps to gather his thoughts.

Detective Kilgarry waited, extending the courtesy he would appreciate if walking in Dickson's shoes.

"Anyway," Derrick continued, "for some reason, Harry Stanton took a liking to me, although not until after I was on the Hill for several years.

"And, you? What did you think of Harry?"

"At first, I considered him someone I could look up to, but, because we served in different parts of Congress, I really didn't have much work with him. It wasn't until about five years ago did Harry begin to seek me out . . ."

Kilgarry scratched a few notes, then returned his attention to the senator. "Interesting choice of words—why did he seek you out?"

"Because he wanted me to join a group of silent investors—that's what he called them—and, he thought I might be interested."

"Were you?"

"Not really—what interested me more was what Harry was up to." A deep sigh. "But, then . . ."

Derrick Dickson's voice caught, something that didn't go unnoticed. Kilgarry gave him a moment, recognizing the senator was grappling with memories. "Take your time . . ."

Dickson sat up a little straighter. "My daughter was kidnapped . . ."

Instantly, Detective Kilgarry cycled through high profile cases in Washington, D.C. within the last five years, and the kidnapping of Dickson's child wasn't one of them. "By whom?"

"Eric Stanton . . ."

Constance adjusted the headphones, checked the sound monitor, then took a long drink of water. Moments later, she clicked 'record.'

An hour gone, she tapped the record icon again, removed the headphones and fluffed her hair, then poured herself a scotch.

Done, and done . .

By the time Colbie finished bringing Detective Daniken up to speed, little doubt remained—it would behoove him to keep her on his side. "So, to make certain I understand you correctly, you want to visit the crime scene . . ."

"Yes—and, I realize your allowing me to do so is against most protocols. But, if I can get in there for a few minutes, I might be able to bring clarity to some of the questions we have . . ."

The detective said nothing for a few seconds, everything in him wanting to deny her request.

But, he couldn't.

Within the hour, both stood in Costin Dalca's master bathroom, each feeling the weight of the space and, for Daniken, it was something he didn't understand. Colbie, however, did. "Can you feel it," she asked, scanning the bathroom for obvious signs of who decided it was time for Costin Dalca to meet his maker. "Whoever did the deed, left one hell of an imprint . . ." Saying such a thing was a calculated risk, but, after their conversation in the car on the way to Dalca's, she knew she could be honest.

"I'm not sure what you mean . . ."

"Well, there's usually some sort of psychic imprint left by the killer—you know, a negative energy of some sort." Colbie leaned up against the bathroom counter, arms crossed. "This is how Dalca stood when he confronted his killer . . ."

The detective was quiet, trying to understand. "You'll have to forgive me—this is my first time working with a psychic." A pause. "So, you're telling me you can see who killed Dalca?"

Colbie shook her head, then turned to the mirror. "Not quite—I see Dalca. Not the killer . . ."

"So . . . do you see Dalca as if he's standing right there?"

A soft chuckle. "No—I see him in my mind's eye." She turned and, in the mirror, she caught a quick glance of the detective—he was trying to understand, but wasn't quite making a go of it. "It's hard to explain," she commented with a smile. "But, as long as I know what's happening, you don't have to!"

"I guess that's a good thing . . ."

Suddenly, Colbie placed her hands on the sides of the expensive, vintage mirror, then closed her eyes. Without prodding, a scene leapt to life—one she knew having to do with Dalca's murder. "He wasn't expecting him . . ."

"Him?"

"Yes—definitely male."

Silence.

"He asked the killer how he got in here . . ."

Detective Daniken began taking notes—chances were good if he didn't, he'd never remember what the petite redhead had to say. "So, he didn't know the killer?"

Again, Colbie was quiet, staring into the mirror.

In uncomfortable silence, the detective said nothing, feeling she would speak when ready.

"Incorrect—he knew the killer."

"Can you tell how the killer entered the house?"

A nod. "Lock pick."

The detective, too, was silent as he tried to figure out how anyone could use a lock pick with surveillance cameras every ten feet. "That doesn't make sense . . ."

What could've been an insult wasn't taken as one, Colbie realizing the reason for his comment. "I think, though it does . . ."

Another, steeping silence.

Finally, she spoke. "Someone helped him—a woman."

"You mean someone else was in the bathroom when Dalca was killed?"

"No—she wasn't here." A pause. "She wasn't in Vegas."

"Then, how . . ."

Suddenly, she took her hands from the mirror, turning to face the detective. "She taught him what to do . . ."

"You mean how to disable the surveillance cameras?"

"Exactly."

"How?"

A deep sigh. "I have no idea . . ."

After a stiff drink or two to calm her nerves, Constance Parnell had one more tough decision to make—throw everyone under the bus, or only Nash Hobbs? Really, when she thought about it, she could simply claim ignorance about specific involvement should someone ask. The real conundrum was, however, would taking such a track offer enough personal satisfaction?

Doubtful.

After a last shot and careful consideration, it seemed wiser and more fulfilling to place her efforts on the political demise of her former employer's son—although, Hobbs was running a pretty close second. But, after considerable thought, she figured there was a possibility of reconciliation.

The question was did she care.

Not really.

Now that she was more educated in the efficacy of electronic surveillance, she possessed a certain expertise valued by those enjoying the political arena.

However, there was another aspect of her situation.

If her partner in crime decided to throw her under the bus, the result would be catastrophic—in her mind, all the more reason to seal his doughy lips. Too risky? Perhaps.

But, what's 'too risky' when it comes to revenge?

"I'm not sure I understand, Senator—you're saying Eric Stanton, Harry Stanton's son, kidnapped your daughter?"

A nod. "When she was fourteen."

"How old is she now?"

"Almost eighteen."

Kilgarry took a deep breath, as if it would somehow make him understand. "I've been around this town for a long time, Sir, and I don't recall such a case . . ."

"That's because we didn't make it a 'case' . . ."

"You didn't report it?"

"No—we took care of it ourselves." The senator didn't take his eyes from the detective. "Can you imagine, Detective? What a mess that would've been?"

As much as Detective Kilgarry didn't want to agree, he had to. "You're right about that . . ." A contemplative pause. "And, Eric Stanton did it?"

"Not directly."

At that moment, Decklin Kilgarry wished he had what the senator was having, but took a drink of water instead. "There were other people involved?"

A nod.

"Care to tell me who?"

"Not quite yet, Detective—I haven't decided if I should leave that to you."

"Wouldn't it be better to slap 'em in jail?"

Dickson snorted slightly before draining his glass. "You don't understand, Detective—what I have to tell you is like a spider web across the country. Lives will change. The country will change . . ."

"Are you telling me it goes to the political pinnacle?"

A smile. "An interesting way to put it—but, to answer your question, yes. Heads will roll, Detective, and I doubt the citizens of this country will put up with what I'm about to tell you . . ."

It was then Decklin reached into his pocket, extracting a small, digital recorder. "Do you mind?"

"Of course not, Detective—my career is already ruined."

CHAPTER 23

Colbie turned again to the mirror, placing her hands on the counter. "I definitely feel as if someone else is involved—I don't think the guy who did this had the know-how."

"So . . . definitely a woman."

She closed her eyes. "Yes."

"You're sure?"

A nod. Then, suddenly, as if a switch flipped and her connection severed, Colbie faced the detective. "That's it—that's all I can see for now."

Detective Daniken wasn't sure what to say—he couldn't really comment on what just happened because he'd never seen such a thing. "Well . . . that was interesting."

Colbie laughed as she headed toward the bedroom. "I can only imagine what you must be thinking!"

"It's probably good you don't know!" He watched as she worked her way around the bed. "Can you tell me anything about the guy who killed him?"

She paused, her fingertips resting lightly on the nightstand. "Tall. Snappy dresser."

"A fashionable kind of guy?"

"Yes, but not really. It's more like that's who he truly was—it's the way he was brought up."

"So, you're saying he came from money?"

"Not necessarily—but, that's what he feels like."

It was then Detective Daniken knew he had to follow the trail. "You've been in D.C.—I'm assuming you know of the man who was murdered in a gated community called 'The Haven.'"

"I heard . . ."

"Do you feel anything about him?"

Colbie's eyebrows arched. "Are you saying there's a connection between Dalca and that guy?"

"I'm not saying anything—just asking." The detective didn't take his eyes from her. "Is there?"

A nod. "There just might be . . ."

Detective Kilgarry pressed a button, then set the digital recorder on the small table between them. "Okay—let's take it from the beginning. How did you learn about your daughter's kidnapping?"

"The usual. A note . . ."

"From whom?"

"At that moment, I didn't know."

"Ransom?"

"No. In fact, it wasn't that type of note, at all—it was typed, of course, but clearly from someone who wanted me to know she was gone."

"An insider?"

A nod. "That was my thought . . ." Dickson took another sip, then placed his glass on the table. "Although, I'm sure the author of the note meant to be cryptic, it wasn't too hard to figure out."

"Why?"

"Because it made me think of a conversation I had with Harry Stanton about two years before Harper was kidnapped—it was the way it was phrased. You know—familiar."

"Do you think it came from Harry?"

"No—but, someone close."

"I take it you're hesitant to name names . . ."

"Indeed—why ruin more lives than I have to, Detective?"

Kilgarry was quiet, trying to figure out why the father of a kidnapped daughter wouldn't report it to the authorities, politician or not. "I have to ask, Senator—other than the press, why didn't you file a report?"

A protracted silence.

"Because I want him all to myself . . ."

Colbie kicked off her shoes, then tapped a quick text to Ryan suggesting they have dinner in and, within the hour, they sat at her small hotel table enjoying two Cobb salads, French bread, and a bottle of merlot. "I kind of felt sorry for him," she commented as she tore off a piece of bread.

"Daniken? Why?"

"Because it was obvious he never witnessed anything like scrying before—in fact, few people have."

"Myself included . . ."

"It's interesting, that's for sure!" She sat back, smile fading, realizing it was time for the conversation she didn't want to have. "I've been giving a lot of thought . . ."

Ryan knew what she was going to say by the apologetic look on her face. "Let me guess—you're not coming back to the firm."

"Like I said, I've been thinking about it for a long time—and, I finally realize I need to do something completely different. If I continue to take cases, I'm never going to explore the other part of me . . ."

Ryan placed his wine glass on the table, then looked her in the eye. "What part is that?" His words laced with an uncustomary sting, he fought to quell his disappointment.

"I have no idea—but, I decided to give up my portion of the firm." With a sigh, her eyes filled with tears. "No need for a buyout . . ."

"All business, huh?"

"C'mon, Ryan—you know that's not the case! I've been thinking about this since Brian died, and you know it!" She paused for a sip, then continued. "There's no enjoyment, anymore—and, spending the rest of my career doing something I don't enjoy doesn't seem particularly fulfilling."

Silence.

"It's only the business—nothing changes between us. We're still the friends we always were . . ."

Ryan's clutching heartbreak burst as he listened. "I understand—I really do." He hesitated, realizing the lump in his throat was the size of Montana. "So, after we wrap up this last case, what are you going to do?"

"Well, I think it's time for me to go back to school . . ."

"You're going back to college?"

"Yes—I'm pretty sure." She eyed him, knowing their conversation was slicing his heart. "In fact, I just heard before meeting for dinner . . ."

A louder silence.

"I'm going to study paranormal psychology at the University of Edinburgh . . ."

"In Scotland?"

Colbie laughed, trying to lighten the mood. "Yes—in Edinburgh, Scotland. They have phenomenal course study, and it's time for me to be who I am." A sip. "You know—who I am at my core."

"Well, nothing I say is going to change your mind—so, all I can do is wish you luck."

"And, visit me in Edinburgh . . ."

"With a name like Fitzpatrick, I guess it would be my stompin' grounds . . ." Gently, he took Colbie's hand. "You know I'm disappointed, but I understand. I really do . . ."

Colbie gave his fingers a squeeze. "I knew you would . . ."

"Are you familiar with Colbie Colleen," Detective Daniken asked his partner as he adjusted the settings on his Zoom screen. "She's a private investigator . . ."

Detective Scanlan shook his head. "Nope—never heard of her."

"I hadn't, either." A pause. "Did you contact Kilgarry?"

"No—I can message him, but he's in Maine for a family wedding. Won't be back until after the weekend . . ."

Daniken said nothing, considering whether he should tell Scanlan about his time with the psychic. "Okay—well, that changes things a bit. But, what I have to say won't wait, so I guess you're my best bet!" He laughed, knowing what he was about to tell his junior detective would blow him out of the water. "Got a pencil and paper?"

"Yep—shoot."

Ryan checked his watch. "It's almost five," he commented as he parked across the street from People's First Delivery.

"My guess is she'll be out the door on the dot," Colbie murmured as she adjusted the binoculars, squinting slightly as she put them to eyes. "And, I'm right—there she is!"

She watched as the twenty-something woman locked the front door, then looked both directions. "She looks like she's expecting someone," Colbie observed. "The third building! She's going to the third building!"

Ryan glanced at her, then pushed the ignition. "I can get you closer . . ."

Within a minute, he eased the car to the far end of the parking lot, offering an unobstructed view of the massive metal-framed building located slightly behind and to the side of the main office. "I'll go," Colbie suggested. "She knows who you are . . ."

"She saw you, too . . ."

But, before Ryan could object further, she was out of the car, skirting the perimeter of the parking lot, fully aware she'd most likely be caught on camera. *But*, she thought, reaching the far side of the building, *it's worth the risk.*

Pausing behind the only palm tree in sight, Colbie scanned the area, taking note of everything outside. Behind the building were two semis—drivers nowhere to be seen—as well as three, detached cargo containers, and a small entry door discreetly located at the rear of the building. Strategically situated surveillance cameras didn't miss a thing, leaving Colbie to abandon any hope of a stealthy approach.

Slowly, she returned to the car as if she were merely taking a walk to stretch her legs.

Moments later, she and Ryan pulled from the parking lot, heading toward the highway—at least, if anyone were watching, that's what they'd probably think. Within a few minutes, however, Ryan circled around and parked across the street, waiting as Colbie kept the binos trained on the building. "I don't like this place," Colbie commented.

Just as Ryan was about to agree, Colbie caught a glimpse of their target at the rear of the building, speaking to whom she and Ryan could only assume was a driver. "They seem pretty comfortable with each other," Ryan muttered. Then, a lingering kiss as the obvious lovebirds parted ways. "Damn it! Nothing more than a workplace romance!"

Both watched as Jessica headed for her car. "Wait for me," Colbie ordered as she hopped out, hoping to intercept her.

Ryan nodded, then watched as Colbie jogged across the parking lot. "Jessica!"

The young woman turned. "Yes?"

Not even a smidge out of breath, Colbie smiled, extending her hand. "If you have a minute, I'd like to ask you a few questions . . ."

Of course, Jessica had no clue she was about to give up everything she knew about Costin Dalca and People's First Delivery, as well as Mihai Bucur—she only recognized Colbie as Mrs. Blickenstaff. "I'm sorry, but we're closed," she apologized, clicking the key fob to her car.

"I promise it'll only take a second," Colbie urged, her smile confident and warm. "Please?"

"Well, okay—what can I do for you?"

Colbie motioned to a bench in a small patch of shade next to the building. "Let's get out of this sun!" A few seconds later, she launched into what she wanted to know. "I'm going to be honest with you," she began. "My name is Colbie, and I'm a private investigator . . ."

"What?"

"Yes—my partner and I were here the first time under the guise of Mr. and Mrs. Blickenstaff."

"Why? Was it something to do with Mr. Dalca's murder?" A brief hesitation. "But, that was before he was murdered . . ."

With that observation, it was clear to Colbie Jessica was an intelligent young woman. "Yes, that's right—but, what I want to talk to you about is Mr. Dalca." She eyed her, hoping the receptionist wouldn't bolt. Then, a tactic she knew would work. "I imagine the cops have been here a few times . . ."

A nod.

"Do they suspect you?"

Suddenly, Jessica's eyes filled with tears. "Me? Why would they suspect me?"

Colbie reached over, patting her hand. "I don't know they do—but, it's a pretty good guess they're checking into anyone and everyone who had anything to do with your boss."

Jessica reached into her pocket, then dabbed at her eyes with a used tissue. "I don't know anything—that's what I told the cops!"

"I believe you!" Colbie waited until the tissue was back in its rightful place. "But, there may be something we're overlooking . . ."

"Like what?"

"Well, let's strip it down to the bare bones—was Mr. Dalca upset about anything recently?'

"Yes—in fact, he was upset when he reviewed the surveillance footage that had you and your hus . . . partner on it."

"Why?"

"He didn't say—but, I do know he ordered Mihai to install a better system immediately."

Colbie was quiet for a few seconds, thinking. "Was there anything about the business you ever thought was strange?"

Jessica cocked her head slightly. "What do you mean by 'strange?'"

"Oh, you know—anything out of the ordinary. Surely, as smart as you are, you keep your eyes peeled. I'm pretty sure I would . . ."

Silence.

"Jessica—I know you've seen things. And, I suspect they aren't good . . ."

"Well . . ."

Colbie waited, watching as the young woman gathered her strength. "If the time comes when you need my help, I'll be there for you . . ."

Well, that did it. Without warning, Jessica Alexandria Mathis dissolved into tears, searching for the tissue again. "I don't know exactly what's going on, but there are deliveries late at night . . ."

"How late?"

"I don't know for sure, but I think it's around midnight— maybe later."

"How do you know?"

"Because my boyfriend and I drive past all the time—we don't live far from here and, when we go by, there's something going on."

"Where? In one of the buildings?"

A nod. "In that one . . ." Jessica pointed to the third building earlier capturing Colbie's interest.

"Have you ever been in it?"

Jessica shook her head. "No! On the first day I worked here, I was told never to go in there."

"Mr. Dalca told you?"

"Yes . . ."

"Did he say why?"

"No—all he said was it was empty, and there was no reason for me to go in. He said I had to stick to the storage building and loading docks."

"Okay—so, how did you know there was something going on in that building?"

"Because the lights were on, and a semi-truck was driving in . . ."

"Into the building?"

"Yes—but, the truck wasn't one of ours."

"You mean it wasn't a People's First truck?"

Another nod.

As Colbie continued to question Jessica gently, there was little doubt she had anything to do with Costin Dalca's murder. "Tell me about the people who are here regularly . . ."

"You mean other than the drivers?"

"Yeah—who do you see all the time?"

Jessica thought for a moment. "Well, no one, really—I mean, no one I think who would kill Mr. Dalca." A pause. "There was one guy, though—I hadn't seen him before, and he seemed to be pretty at home as he walked around."

"What did he look like?"

"Tall. Really tall—and, he reminded me of an older male model. You know, the kind who can wear anything . . ."

Colbie grinned. "Wouldn't that be nice? I always need to have things shortened!"

Finally, Jessica smiled. "I'm exactly the opposite!"

So, for the next fifteen minutes or so, Colbie and Jessica chatted about the inner workings of People's First Delivery— at least, what Jessica knew of it. By the time they parted, Colbie knew exactly who Jessica noticed casually strolling around the company's premises. "No doubt in my mind," she commented to Ryan after returning to the car.

He watched as she buckled her seat belt, then took out a small notepad from her bag. "Remember the guy I saw," she asked as she wrote quickly, "walking around the first time we were here?"

"Kind of—as we were leaving, if I recall."

"Yes—at the time I had no idea of who he was."

"Now?"

She turned to look at him. "None other than Walker Newton . . "

CHAPTER 24

*A*s wedded bliss continued to sour in the Stanton household, the discord was enough to make Elaine seriously rethink her life, as well as how she wanted it go.

Living under Eric Stanton's thumb wasn't it.

Even so, there was little she could do—or, so she thought until a serendipitous meeting with Constance Parnell in front of the cucumbers in the natural food market. Of course, neither really had anything to say to the other since they didn't travel in the same circles—but, to be kind, Elaine invited her for tea and, shortly after making it through the checkout line, both sat in the afternoon shade on Elaine

Stanton's veranda enjoying the fruits of Elaine's morning labor. "I swear, Elaine, you are the best cook! Eric's a lucky man!"

Blushing and pleased, Elaine thanked her, comfortable with the accolades until conversation turned to her husband. "What's it like," Constance asked as she reached for another tasty treat.

"I don't know what you mean . . ."

"Oh, you know—living as a Stanton. I often thought it would be difficult to live under Harry's thumb—it's no secret he was a difficult man." A pause. "So, I wondered if it's the same living with Eric . . ."

"Well, it's not particularly easy, if that's what you mean."

Constance eyed her with one eyebrow arching. "Don't you ever wonder what we talk about in our meetings?"

"It's none of my business."

"Is that what Eric tells you?" It was obvious by her tone, Constance Parnell had little patience for a man who chose to exact power in myriad, subliminal ways.

"No, but what do I need to know?" Suddenly, Elaine's tone changed as she reached for the teapot. "What are you getting at, Constance? Is there something you feel compelled to tell me?"

Constance was quiet for a few moments, thinking about what she set in motion only a few days prior. If everything went according to plan, Detective Kilgarry would receive a thumb drive detailing Eric Stanton's little side business—one promoted and funded by Harry until Eric could manage things on his own.

But, when the despicable senator croaked?

All hell.

Decklin Kilgarry grabbed a Guinness from the fridge, kicked off his shoes, then parked his butt on the couch in front of the television without turning it on. Still reeling from his conversation with Derrick Dickson, he wasn't quite certain where to pick up his investigation given the apparent intricacies involved. Of course, everything the senator told him couldn't be verified since there was no investigation into Dickson's daughter's kidnapping. *But,* he thought after taking his first drink, *judging from the way he was acting? A man wronged . . .*

There was, of course, the possibility the senator was playing the role of a lifetime with the hope of achieving something he considered valuable. Chances of that happening, however? *Negligible . . .*

Determined to discover who offed Walker Newton, there was no doubt in the detective's mind. *Stanton's wife knows something, and I'll be damned if I won't find out what it is—and, if Eric Stanton is capable of what Dickson says he is?*

With that thought he downed half of his beer, then opened file folders with personal notes regarding Walker's case. Again, he listened to the interview with Nash Hobbs, solidifying his gut feeling that Dickson was, indeed, telling the truth. *The rough part,* he considered as he figured out his next investigative move, *will be interviewing Harper Dickson.*

If that's possible . . .

Putting logistics of such a possibility aside, he turned to the main players in Eric Stanton's ring of what was turning out to be despicable politicians. Never suspecting their long-standing atrocities against young women, what Kilgarry knew by the time he called it a night was Eric Stanton was on a short leash.

Real short . . .

"I think, Elaine, it's time you know everything . . ." Constance placed her teacup on its saucer, then wiped her mouth with a napkin crafted of Italian linen.

"You sound as if you have a secret to tell—although, I have no idea why you think it concerns me."

Constance Parnell smiled, slightly amused by Elaine's false naïveté. "Oh, but it does—and, I think when you hear what I have to say, you'll agree it may be time to consider a life change."

"A life change? Oh, please—I'm perfectly happy where I am. Eric is very good to me . . ."

It was then Constance decided a delicate touch wouldn't be nearly as satisfying as the direct approach. "What do you know of your husband's . . . side business?"

"Side business? Other than being a politician?"

A nod.

Elaine leveled a look at her guest, one similar to the one she launched at Walker Newton right before his— well, 'untimely demise' probably describes it best. "I'm sure whatever you're referring to is absolutely false—Eric has no 'side business.'" Another scorching glare. "I think it's time for you to go, Constance . . ."

With that, Constance Parnell stood, picked up her keys and handbag, then pushed in her chair as her mama taught her to always do. "Then, I wish you luck, Elaine . . ."

Derrick Dickson dressed in the morning quiet, carefully measuring what he needed to accomplish—if things were to go according to plan, he needed to be in place no later than thirty minutes after the false dawn.

Eric Stanton is a man of habit, he thought as he checked his pockets for his keys, finally locating them on the kitchen counter next to the coffee pot. *All the better for me . . .*

And, indeed, he was right.

By the time he arrived at the Stanton estate, soft lights were on, the signal for a new day dawning. As he watched from the bushes lining the driveway, it was then Derrick needed to make a choice—confront Stanton on his own turf, hoping for a confession? Or, simply take care of matters without any fuss? Naturally, Dickson would be recording every word without Eric's knowledge just in case he happened to get lucky enough to catch Stanton in a moment of weakness accompanied by loose lips.

It was a tough decision, too—Dickson waited a long time to exact the revenge Stanton so richly deserved. As far as he was concerned, there was little reason for Harry's son to draw another breath—but, when really thinking about it, placing a few rounds would be the easy way out. No— Derrick would rather have him suffer.

Just like his daughter did during the most terrifying few days of her life.

"So, if Walker Newton offed Dalca, then who offed him?" Ryan glanced at Colbie, quickly returning his attention to his laptop. "There's not much in the press . . ."

"Daniken mentioned they're keeping a low profile—but, I have a feeling things are about to shift in our direction."

"Because?"

Colbie watched as he typed for a few seconds, then gave her the go-ahead to continue. "After spending time at Dalca's, there was something bugging me, but I couldn't figure it out." A pause. "With Dalca dead, it makes me wonder if there's been a hiccup in People's First's operations . . ."

"You mean who's driving the bus if Dalca's no more?"

"Yes—it doesn't feel as if anything's changed. Business as usual—and, I also got the feeling someone who's already on our radar is involved somehow."

"Do you know who?"

"Not really—I mean, I don't think Jessica has anything to do with it, so that leaves Mihai Bucur and Eric Stanton."

Ryan was quiet, thinking of his conversation with Colbie after she returned from her investigation with Daniken. "Didn't you tell me something about the surveillance cameras?"

"Yes—why?"

"And, didn't you mention there was a woman involved?"

Colbie nodded, waiting for her partner to continue.

"Okay—so, remember when we were doing our first surveillance, and we were staking out the Stanton's?"

"Of course . . ."

"Think back—what struck us strange?"

"The dark blue car."

Ryan smiled, opting not to take advantage of the opportunity to dish out a dig. "That's right—and, remember Jake said he saw it not too long ago?"

"That's right! Constance Parnell!" A long pause as Colbie tried to work out what wasn't making sense. "But, what would she have to do with Costin Dalca?"

"I'm not sure—but, she's the only woman in Stanton's circle, not to mention she was Harry's assistant for years. There has to be some sort of allegiance . . ."

"You're probably right about that—and, we've given her little credence during our investigation. Maybe it's time we do a little digging into Constance Parnell's history—what do you think?"

"My thought, exactly."

By the time Detective Kilgarry pulled out the chair to his desk, he was two coffees in and it wasn't quite seven. "Package," Marsh announced as he tossed a padded envelope on his boss's desk, frowning, recognizing the look of little sleep. "You look like shit . . ."

Kilgarry laughed, snatched the envelope, then took out a letter opener from a cracked coffee mug housing most of his pens. "Always good to know you're on my side, Marsh!"

Out of an abundance of caution, the detective peered inside before extracting a small thumb drive—then, he checked the envelope. "No return address . . ."

"Of course not! You didn't really expect one, did you?" Marsh watched as Kilgarry fitted the drive into his computer.

"Not really . . ." Leaning back in his chair as prompts on the screen directed him to open the file, suddenly, a voice greeted him. "Hello, Detective Kilgarry—my name is Constance Parnell."

Both men were quiet as the voice continued. "I hope you have a cup of coffee because what I'm about to tell you will take awhile. It'll also rock your world . . ."

Kilgarry clicked the pause icon. "Ever heard of her?"

"Nope . . ."

Another click. "And," the voice continued, "before you waste your time running a check, I was Senator Harry Stanton's assistant for twenty-six years . . ." A pause, perhaps waiting for gasps or raised eyebrows to subside. "And, I have a story to tell . . ."

So, for the next hour, Detectives Kilgarry and Marsh listened, neither commenting as they scribbled feverishly on their legal pads and, at the end of the recording, both looked at each other, stunned. "There's the connection with People's First Delivery in Vegas," Detective Marsh finally commented.

Kilgarry nodded, attempting to completely digest all of Constance Parnell's information. "She said there's more— but, if she's as smart as I think, she won't give us anything until we promise immunity."

"Agreed—a mistake she wouldn't make."

Suddenly, Decklin got up and grabbed his jacket from the back of his office door. "Get her address—it's time the three of us have a little chat."

The moment a man finds out he's actually a coward is never a good day, undoubtedly leaving him to question his manhood and everything else in life. So, by the time Derrick Dickson arrived on Capitol Hill?

His day had already taken a downward turn.

As much as he wanted to stand in front of Eric Stanton with the barrel of his Smith & Wesson pointed at his forehead, he couldn't do it.

He just couldn't do it.

And, other than sacrificing the satisfaction of blowing away the man who was responsible for his daughter's kidnapping, the consequences were simply too dire. *I'll let Kilgarry take care of it,* he thought as he climbed the steps to the second floor, the echo of his shoes on the marble steps punctuating momentary self-loathing.

I've done all I can do . . .

Elaine listened as her husband started his car, then pulled slowly out of the garage, stopping only for a moment to adjust his rearview mirror.

Then?

Quietly, as if someone lurked in the shadows, she opened her husband's library door, scanning the room, deciding what she wanted to tackle first. Other than serving his guests on occasion, it was the one room in the house where she wasn't allowed, Eric keeping his secrets under lock and key. *Not anymore,* she thought, plucking a small key from her apron pocket. *Now, it's just a matter of seeing where it fits . . .*

Actually, Elaine had access to her husband's inner sanctum for quite some time after discovering the key tucked away in his underwear drawer accompanied by a sticky note with numbers written on it in Eric's hand. In a moment of delirious glee when she realized what she discovered, Elaine had a copy of the key made within the hour, squirreling it away where he'd never find it. She did realize, however, if discovered, invasion of his privacy would result in what she could no longer endure. So, when Constance Parnell started flapping her jaws?

It made Elaine think.

If she were the one to expose her husband's nefarious business associations and dealings, it wasn't a stretch to convince Washington's finest of Eric's responsibility regarding Walker Newton's unfortunate end of life.

Was it?

It makes sense, she thought as she tried fitting the key in her husband's desk drawers with no luck. Then, as if the heavens smiled upon her, she spied a small fire safe tucked below the bottom shelf of the built-ins on the far wall from the door.

Armed with the sticky note, carefully she tried the combination and, with little effort, the safe's door opened to reveal much less than she expected—a pistol, three manila file folders, a wad of cash, and a lock box.

Standard for a Stanton.

Gently, she closed the safe door, spun the lock, then crossed to the window behind his desk. It wasn't beyond her husband to show up unexpectedly under the guise of leaving something behind. But, Elaine knew . . .

He was checking.

Standing just to the side of the open drapes, she scanned their front yard and driveway. *Not today, Eric . . .*

Not today.

CHAPTER 25

I's always thrilling when a case comes together, and Colbie was seldom wrong when it came to feeling an end was on the horizon. "We're close," she commented as she and Ryan met for coffee on their first day back in D.C. "I got a call from Daniken this morning, telling me the Washington investigator assigned to Walker Newton's murder has information for him."

"Did he say what?"

"No—he had to get to a meeting, but he'll call later to fill me in."

"Who's on it here?"

"Kilgarry. Decklin Kilgarry . . ."

"Never heard of him . . ."

"Neither have I—but, there's no reason for our paths to cross. All I know is he's investigating Walker Newton— which means sooner or later he's going to be investigating Eric Stanton."

"If he isn't already," Ryan agreed. "However, with what we know now, I think we know the whole story . . ."

"Maybe—right now, though, we need to concentrate on Constance Parnell. What have you learned?"

"Nothing outstanding—she was Senator Harry Stanton's assistant for over two decades, seemingly dedicating her life to him and his work in Congress."

"It says that?"

Ryan grinned. "Yep—in an interview from seven years ago. She said it's her calling to serve . . ."

"Oh, please . . ." Colbie focused on her partner. "Not only does that sound hokey, I feel as if she's lying."

"Maybe she is—but, we'll probably never know. So, in the meantime, I'm going to keep on her today to see where she goes . . ."

"Is she working anywhere?"

Ryan shrugged, then closed his laptop. "If you don't have anything else, I'm out. I'm going to hang out at the Capitol to see if she shows up since I couldn't watch her place from first thing this morning. I'll do that tomorrow . . ." He stood, then threw fifteen bucks on the table. "What about you?"

"I think it's time I get to know Elaine Stanton . . ."

"Constance Parnell?"

"Yes—I've been expecting you." She stepped aside, allowing the detectives to enter. "Please, have a seat . . ."

Detectives Kilgarry and Marsh followed her into a tiny living room appointed with overstuffed furniture and vintage fringed lamps. For some reason, the decor was what he expected—what threw him was the wall of electronic equipment and gadgets, all appearing state-of-the-art.

"I'm sure you know why we're here, Ms. Parnell . . ."

Constance smiled, noticing Detective Marsh was paying more attention to her wall of toys than their conversation. "I thought it might interest you, Detective . . ."

Decklin was quiet for a moment, assessing who sat across from him. At first glance, she seemed a woman of hard work, but, certainly there was much more. "I'm curious, Ms. Parnell . . ."

Another smile. "I imagine you are . . ."

"Why are you putting yourself in such a position? What you chose to divulge will place you in the media crosshairs once the story gets out."

"I know—but, as you've no doubt guessed, I must maintain my standing, Detective Kilgarry. What Harry Stanton did was reprehensible and, after lurking in the shadows for as long as I did, it was time to stop thinking about myself."

Bullshit?

Of course.

The truth was she wanted to see Harry Stanton's reputation fried and his son in the hoosegow for the rest of his years, and it had nothing to do with anyone else—what happened to him from that day forward was none of her business. Even those young girls whom Eric befriended on nights when he couldn't sleep? The promises he made?

None of it mattered.

What mattered was how Harry Stanton shattered her life, making her believe she was worth absolutely nothing, treating her like something on the bottom of his shoe. Honestly? She wouldn't have stayed with him for as long as she did if it weren't for the money—and, an extra chunk of it was for keeping her mouth shut about affairs best kept undisclosed. In fact, she became a confidant of sorts, always available when he needed her—but, after twenty-six years of sacrificing her self-respect, enough was enough, and it was time for Harry to pay the price. After all, she had a nice little nest egg socked away for her future—why shouldn't she take matters into her own hands?

If only he hadn't dropped dead eating a ham and cheese sandwich, she thought waiting for the detective's next question.

Kilgarry didn't take his eyes from her. "What haven't you told us, Ms. Parnell?"

Eyes narrowing and leveling a look of nothing less than pure contempt, her gaze met the detective's—and, it was then the true Constance Parnell showed up to the party. "What I haven't told you, Detective? Why, who else is involved, of course!"

Then?

Names.

"Mrs. Stanton? I'm sorry to bother you. My name is Colbie Colleen—I'm wondering if you have a few moments?"

Elaine stared at the petite redhead on her doorstep wondering who the hell Colbie Colleen was and why was she there. "I'm sorry—do I know you?"

An engaging smile. "No—you've never laid eyes on me in your life!" Another grin. "But, if you have five minutes, I'll appreciate it . . ."

What Elaine Stanton instinctively realized as she stood face-to-face with the woman who could ruin everything?

Opportunity just came a knockin'.

She wasn't, however, about to invite her in—the front porch would be just fine. "What can I do for you?"

Fully realizing she wouldn't have the opportunity to see more than the yard, Colbie offered her appreciation with a handshake. "As I said, my name is Colbie—and, I'm investigating illegal trafficking in the United States."

As Colbie shook Elaine's hand, her fingers tingled as she tapped into the energy and, at that moment, her investigation coalesced. Without question, she knew which direction she needed to go.

"Good heavens! What would I know about something like that?"

"That's what I need to find out . . ."

Elaine managed a reserved smirk, thrilled with her luck. Opportunity didn't knock just once . . .

It knocked twice.

"Perhaps we should discuss this inside . . ."

Moments later, Elaine sat across from Colbie, hands folded in her lap, obviously innocent of whatever the redheaded stranger was about to bring up. "What do you want to know?"

But, before Colbie could dive into the intricacies of her investigation, there was one thing she wanted to know. "Well, I'm not even sure you can help me . . ." Then, an innocent act of her own. "What's it like being the wife of a famous senator?"

"Eric? Famous?" A soft chuckle. "I wouldn't exactly say that . . ."

"Really? Even after . . ."

A quizzical look. "Even after what, Ms. Colleen?"

Colbie sighed gently, as if troubled by what she were about to say. "Well, you know—the whole Vegas thing."

Elaine was quiet as she struggled to understand. "I'm afraid I don't understand—what 'Vegas thing?'"

As Colbie watched every expression, one thing became instantly clear.

Elaine Stanton had no idea.

"After Harry died, Detective, it wasn't long until his son approached me with a deal he thought I couldn't refuse—and, in some ways, I suppose I couldn't. But, not because of reasons he surmised—he figured I'd be delighted to have a significant income in the wake of my no longer having a job."

"Were you?"

A snicker. "I didn't need his money—but, to achieve my goal, I needed something else."

"What was that?"

"Information, Detective—information."

"Were you seeking something specific?"

Constance paused for a few seconds, weighing her options for the umpteenth time. While there was no backing out of her original story submitted to the detective on a thumb drive, she could limit what she wanted him to know. Before that, however?

Time to negotiate.

"Before we continue, Detective, I think we should understand the parameters of our conversation. As you now know, I have information that can bring down half of Congress—information you need."

Kilgarry tried not to smile. "Let me guess—immunity?"

"Of course."

"I can't make any promises . . ."

After considering his response for a moment, Constance stood. "Then, I'm afraid our conversation is over, Detective." A pause. "But, I offer an open door, should you change your mind . . ."

"I simply meant it will take time."

"I understand—the ever-turning 'wheels of justice.'" Then, she motioned toward the front door. "As I said, Detective, my offer stands should you return with an offer of complete immunity . . ."

Kilgarry said nothing until he stood beside her, the open door providing a welcomed puff of fresh air. "Clearly, Ms. Parnell, you're an intelligent woman. I suggest thinking about how much time you're willing to serve . . ."

A laugh. "Oh, I don't think so—I have information you want, so you'll be back." She paused, smiling. "Perhaps, we'll have tea . . ."

With that, she closed the door behind both detectives, certain they left without gaining the upper hand. *Well played, Constance,* she congratulated herself.

Well played . . .

Parked just down the street from Constance Parnell's apartment, Ryan watched as Detectives Kilgarry and Marsh headed to their car. *Who the hell are those guys,* he wondered, keeping the binos trained on them until they drove from sight, his gut telling him they were cops.

He smiled as he recalled Colbie's words years prior. "When you're surveilling someone, she suggested, "never leave right away. It's a good bet the parade isn't over . . ."

Again, he trained the binos on the entrance to Constance Parnell's apartment, a minute or two later the wisdom of his partner's words ringing true. Keeping her in sight as she locked the front door then headed to her car, he scribbled notes while steadying the binos with his free hand, barely glancing at his tablet.

Without looking in the rearview mirror, she pulled onto the street, then headed into traffic, making it easy for Ryan to follow without detection.

Thirty minutes later?

What he could only surmise was a cozy tête-à-tête with Nash Hobbs.

CHAPTER 26

*A*s soon as Colbie mentioned Las Vegas, Elaine Stanton instantly recognized the elusive door of opportunity was starting to squeak open. Of course she knew about Eric's business dealings in Vegas—at least what he told her—although, the more she thought about it, the more that was coming into question.

"I think," Colbie prompted, "it's time we stopped beating around the bush, don't you, Mrs. Stanton?" Without waiting for an answer, she continued. "Your husband is involved in a human trafficking ring involving young girls, and it's operating out of Las Vegas . . ."

"I don't . . ."

"Please—let's get past the false denial and any righteous indignation that may be forthcoming. Your husband—and, perhaps, you—will undoubtedly serve prison time when it comes to light, and you're rightfully prosecuted."

Then, Colbie waited.

It was interesting watching the stately, middle-aged woman's face blanch to the color of bleached flour. If there were any doubt she knew what her husband was up to, it vanished within seconds.

Suddenly, Elaine's face set and her life became one of survival. "I don't know what Eric was—and, is—up to, Ms. Colleen. The sad fact is I've always suspected the worst of my husband, but more so within the last several years . . ." A step across the threshold of that door of opportunity.

"Before Harry died?"

A nod. "Yes. Well before . . ."

"Do you know Costin Dalca?"

A temptation to lie rose in Elaine's throat, receding only when she realized the gravity of her situation. "Yes—I know of him."

"Walker Newton?"

Another nod. "Yes. But, not personally."

"Did your husband have anything to do with the murder of Costin Dalca or Walker Newton?"

"'And' Walker Newton . . ."

Colbie struggled to not show her surprise regarding the ease with which Lady Stanton threw her husband under the bus. "How do you know?"

A momentary silence. "He told me."

Of course, that was a lie. Eric Stanton never confided in his wife about anything, let alone committing two murders. If there were one thing he knew, it was his wife's propensity for blabbing to the wrong people. Truth be known, that was why he preferred to keep her under wraps much of the time, quashing any opportunity to open her mouth.

"Did your husband actually murder them himself," Colbie asked.

Elaine shook her head. "I doubt it. One thing about my husband? He doesn't like getting his hands dirty—that's why he hired Walker Newton." An icy stare. "Let's be clear about one thing, Ms. Colleen—Eric Stanton is capable of anything in order to achieve whatever he deems important." A pause. "Usually, it has to do with money . . ."

As Colbie digested what she was hearing, Elaine couldn't help thinking the conversation was going in her direction—her favor. It was a position of power she enjoyed as she acquiesced to the delight she felt while backing up the bus for another run. The phrase 'just desserts' came to mind, although Elaine never was one to gloat.

"Why did your husband murder Costin Dalca and Walker Newton?"

"Like I said, it isn't Eric's nature to do such undesirable work himself. I believe—although, I'm not one hundred percent certain, it makes more sense for Walker Newton do the dirty work."

"So, you're saying Walker Newton murdered Costin Dalca as directed by your husband, Eric Stanton—is that correct? If that's the case, I'm not sure I understand why . . ."

"Because the noose is tightening, Ms. Colleen—Eric got word of a . . . well, mutiny, I guess you'd call it. Up until several months ago, everything was going fine—until Eric began worrying about one of the senators."

"What do you mean?"

"Eric was afraid one of his colleagues was on to him . . ."

It was then everything clicked. "Do you know who?"

A nod. "Jake Powers."

You know when clouds part and choirs sing? When you know the truth? Well, it was then Colbie knew she was right to head to Washington unannounced months prior. Realizing her friend was being set up, there was a certain satisfaction when following her gut. Even so, something didn't feel right.

Something she didn't quite understand.

"When did you know about your husband's involvement in the trafficking ring?"

"Several years ago—but, it wasn't until Derrick Dickson's daughter was in the wrong place at the wrong time did I see his true intent."

"Which was?"

"Extortion—money. Power." A pause. "And, you know as well as I, Ms. Colleen, when power is involved, the more people want it."

"Who's involved?"

Without so much as a blink, Elaine Stanton squared her shoulders, well aware of what she was about to do. "Well, my husband, of course—Harry, too, until he died—Nash Hobbs, Constance Parnell, and Walker Newton. There are others, of course, but those are the main players . . ."

Again, Colbie was quiet, thinking. "But," if you knew about this all along, why didn't you speak up?"

"Because doing so is a death wish . . ." Elaine hesitated, then continued. "That's why—when Derrick Dickson's daughter was kidnapped for my husband's pleasure—I knew I had to do something."

"But, that was a several years ago . . ."

"Yes, but you know how slowly politics move, Ms. Colleen. My husband's agenda to make millions while throwing the lives of innocents in the trash was, indeed, more than I could bear. But, I valued my life . . ."

"You said you had to do something . . ."

Elaine nodded, lifting her chin slightly, as if her actions should be lauded in some way. "Yes. I wrote a note to Senator Dickson, letting him know of his daughter's location."

"And, I assume, that action saved your daughter?"

"Yes—although, she's still traumatized."

"I can well imagine . . ."

As she listened, Colbie didn't realize the tension building in her shoulders and neck. What Elaine Stanton was telling her rang true and—with what Colbie knew about Dickson's embedding in Stanton's circle—it made a lot more sense. Even so, Colbie had no doubt Eric Stanton's wife was lying about something.

She just had to figure out what it was . . .

"You were right . . ." Constance dipped her teabag three times in her cup, then gracefully draped the string with the tag off its rim, allowing it to steep. "They just left."

As much as Constance wasn't wild about keeping company with Mr. Hobbs for much longer, she realized the importance of sticking to a plan and keeping a clear mind. As soon as Kilgarry left Nash prior to his conversation with her, Hobbs was on the phone instructing her in the finer points of deflecting suspicion. If that didn't work, Plan B was making themselves look like children with halos.

Although he knew nothing of her recent change of heart toward him, he suspected and, as unbecoming as it may seem, he stopped at nothing to rectify the situation. "Did you mention me?"

"Of course not—I didn't mention anyone. In fact, other than what I revealed on the thumb drive, they left without knowing a thing."

Hobbs was quiet, mentally cycling through his plan. After his last meeting with Eric Stanton he kept a low profile, refusing to call further attention to himself—and, when he really crunched the details, there was nothing pointing to him when it came to the corruption within congressional walls. All he did?

A little investigating.

That's it.

Constance glared at him from across the small table. "We're in this up to our eyeball—for both of us, immunity is the only way out."

"I know that—don't forget it was my idea in the first place. In my line of business, I know how cops work and, when they come crawling, there'll be a price to pay . . ."

"So, what's next?"

Hobbs met her glare with one of his own. "Like I told you—the ball's in their court."

By late evening, Colbie was ready to call it a day, her energy at a low ebb. Ryan popped in for a minute for a quick debrief, then headed to his room to catch up on much needed sleep. For Colbie?

Shuteye wasn't in the cards.

Good thing, too, since Detective Daniken called well after what should've been anyone's bedtime. "I'm sorry to wake you," he apologized as soon as she answered.

Colbie laughed, then flicked on the nightstand light. "You're lucky—I couldn't sleep!"

"Good—I won't keep you, but I want to let you know I just talked to Detective Kilgarry out there, and he said he's pretty sure Walker Newton whacked Dalca. All he needs to do now is put the pieces together."

"I think he's right . . ."

Daniken chuckled. "You know something. Tell me . . ."

So, for the next thirty minutes they discussed the salient points of their cases, Colbie filling him in on her conversation with Elaine, both agreeing she was ripe for spilling her guts. "She's a tough woman," Colbie commented. "But, she's wounded—and, those wounds are a mile wide and a mile deep."

"Abuse?"

"I suspect so, although she didn't say as much. Just a feeling . . ."

Both were quiet, each knowing the damage spousal abuse causes. "Do you think she's involved," Daniken finally asked.

Colbie nodded, although he couldn't see. "Yep."

"Why?"

"Because when I was talking to her, I heard two gunshots."

"What?"

A smile. "Not actual shots . . ." She paused, trying to figure out a way to explain it. Finally, she gave up. "It's psychic thing . . ."

"Ah—so, what does that mean?"

It's always tricky when trying to place someone in a certain situation without anything but conjecture to back it up—and, Colbie new what she was about to say would have to hold water sooner or later. "I can't prove it, but I think she has something to do with Walker Newton's murder . . ."

"Based on?"

"Like I said, it's a feeling. But, as the wife of an attorney and statesman, she would certainly know a wife can't testify against her husband. So, that would be score one for him when it comes to prosecution . . ."

"True, but if we can link Stanton to Costa's murder by proving he was the one calling the shots, he's toast, anyway."

"You're probably right—but, I think there are a whole bunch of higher ups involved, and when this comes out?"

"When it comes out, maybe it'll shake things up out there—God knows this kind of prurient corruption can't be allowed to continue!"

Colbie thought for a moment, considering the least of possible consequences. "It's corruption at its finest, that's for sure . . ."

"And, from the sound of it, personal gratification and money is their only agenda . . ."

"Don't forget power," Colbie commented as they were about to end their call. "It's deceptively alluring—all we can hope for is having a strong enough case against everyone involved to bring them down. That's it—we can't do any more."

The detective agreed. "God willing . . ."

CHAPTER 27

*D*etective Kilgarry didn't look up—in fact, he didn't look up until Nash Hobbs pulled back the chair from in front of the detective's desk, sat down, then waited for some sort of acknowledgment. "What do you want, Marsh," the detective asked.

"Nothing yet, unless you'd like to put me on the force." Hobbs tried not to smile as he watched the detective's expression. "But, I'm probably too old . . ."

Kilgarry smiled, then leaned back in his chair, eyeing the private detective. "You are too old—what do you want, Hobbs?"

"It's come to my attention you had a conversation with Constance Parnell . . ."

"Yes . . ."

"Well, I think I can add to what Constance had to say—but, of course, with the same caveat."

"Immunity."

"Exactly. And, when you hear what I have to say, you'll understand why . . ."

Kilgarry was quiet, considering how many he would lose to the immunity gig if he wanted to get to the bottom of a human trafficking ring funded by none other than members of the United States congress. "I'll tell you the same thing I told Ms. Parnell—I can't promise."

"Come now, Detective—you and I know you've already made arrangements. Isn't that true?"

The detective said nothing, clearly understanding he wasn't sitting across from someone who was wet behind the ears when it came to the rough side of life, as well as the way of precinct politics and protocols. "How can I be sure your information is worth it?"

"You can't. But, as with any case as despicable as yours, concessions must be made—don't you agree?"

As much as Kilgarry didn't want to admit it, Hobbs was right. With a gut feeling and a prayer, when discussing it with those on the ladder a few rungs higher than himself, he secured the immunity offer to those he thought deserving. "Just use your discretion wisely," his boss cautioned. "Know what you're paying for . . ."

"Perhaps." A pause. "I'm a busy man, Mr. Hobbs—are we going to have a meaningful discussion, or dance around what you think may be important?"

Hobbs smiled, enjoying the banter of two whose professions were closely related. "Immunity, then?"

Silence. Then, only one word. "Granted."

"Constance?"

"The same—granted."

"Excellent—I suggest you get your pad and pencil ready. You're going to need it."

"I'll do better than that," Kilgarry smiled, pushing a small recorder to the middle of his desk.

As Detective Marsh passed by the detective's office, his boss motioned to him. "If you don't mind, I'd like to have Detective Marsh join us . . ."

Another smile. "Of course, I don't mind . . ." A platitude? Yes. But, a necessary one since Hobbs knew an objection wouldn't make a damned bit of difference. "Feel free to record," he added wryly as he shifted in his chair to keep his left leg from going to sleep—'circulation issues' his doctor tagged it.

Within a minute or two, Detective Marsh was settled against the wall behind Hobbs, Kilgarry tapping the record button. "Okay, Mr. Hobbs, thank you for coming in—as I understand it, you'd like to speak about . . ."

"My involvement with shipments of illegals through Las Vegas—People's First Delivery—spearheaded by Eric Stanton, and operated by Costin Dalca and Mihai Bucur."

Kilgarry scribbled a few notes while Detective Marsh kept a wary eye on Nash Hobbs. "In other words," Kilgarry prompted, "human trafficking—is that correct?"

A nod. "When it came to my attention, I found Mr. Stanton's—and, other's—actions reprehensible, and I knew I was in a position to do something about it. But, when I learned of Senator Dickson's daughter?" Another pause. "Well, let's just say that shed a new light on things . . ."

More notes. "Continue . . ."

"As I said, when I learned of Eric Stanton's abducting Harper Dickson, it turned my stomach—so, I set out to position myself within his organization."

"Organization? Consisting of . . ."

"Well, at the time, the most notable were, of course, Senator Harry Stanton and his son. As time went on, several more joined, each hoping for massive payouts depending on where the cargo was placed."

"Cargo?"

Nash Hobbs nodded. "Exactly what the Stantons called them, Detective." He paused, recalling the enormity of the trafficking operation. "Senators and House reps are making millions on the sly, never considering anything but their own prurient interests." Another pause. "Make no mistake, Detective, power and money is the only thing driving many of our esteemed politicians, and no one has the guts to strike down their personal and political agendas."

"Until now, Mr. Hobbs?" As much as Kilgarry wanted to believe every word, the experienced detective knew better. "Why now? You weren't so eager to speak to me when I visited you the first time . . ."

"I understand your reluctance to believe me, Detective—I would, too, if I were your shoes. But, I assure you, what I'm telling you is, indeed, true."

Kilgarry glanced at Marsh, took a drink of water, then reviewed his notes for a few seconds. "Where does Constance Parnell fit into all of this?"

Hobbs smiled, recalling the first time they met. "I had no idea who she was until I began investigating Harry Stanton—and, after ingratiating myself to him and his cause by offering my investigative services, I met Constance. After spending only a few minutes with her, it was clear she hated Harry's guts and—as any good investigator would—I figured she could be of benefit . . ."

"If you only spent a minimal amount of time with her, how do you know she hated Harry?"

"Just a feeling, Detective. It was the way she looked at him—the edge in her voice when bowing to his demands. You know what I mean . . ."

Kilgarry didn't confirm or deny. "Go on . . ."

Again, Hobbs shifted in his chair. "So, I got to know her—and, I was right. Constance Parnell hates Harry Stanton's guts as well as everyone in his family."

"Including Elaine?"

"Especially her—Constance knows damned well Elaine Stanton is well aware of her husband's business dealings—and, other proclivities, as well. But, she puts up with it . . ." Hobbs hesitated, hating what he was about to reveal. "It's no secret, Detective, that Elaine Stanton is a battered wife. What happens behind closed doors we'll never truly know, but when we met at Stanton's home?"

Detective Kilgarry watched the private investigator closely, noting a flicker of sadness in his eyes. "What happened at Stanton's, Mr. Hobbs?"

"Well, all of us noticed the swollen and discolored black eyes, although she did her best to disguise it. Constance, in particular, hated Eric all the more for it, often telling me he's just like Harry."

"Is he?"

"Peas in a pod, Detective. Peas in a pod . . ."

With the scent of unfinished business staking its claim, Colbie didn't hesitate to again appear on Elaine Stanton's doorstep unannounced. Experience proved surprise tactics were, indeed, the best approach, so, when Eric's wife opened the door, Colbie greeted her like an old friend. "Elaine! It's me! I hope you don't mind, but I took a chance on your being home—do you have a few minutes?" A smile. "I promise! Only a few minutes . . ."

Well, what could've been a distinct disadvantage morphed into another serendipitous opportunity. "Of course! Please come in!"

So, again, they sat, Elaine as nervous as the first time even though she thought it didn't show. "When I was here a few days ago," Colbie began, "when I left, I felt as if something were missing."

Elaine's wide-eyed innocence was almost convincing. "Missing? I don't know what you mean . . ."

"Well, to be frank, I don't think you told me everything."

Then, the shift. Elaine's back straightened as it often did when confronted with something she chose not to like, Colbie noticing the senator's wife lifted her chin a little higher. "But, why should I? When you think about it, Ms. Colleen, I don't have to tell you anything . . ."

Certainly, that was true—but, clamming up didn't fit her plan. "You're right, of course," Colbie agreed. "But, I know you don't condone your husband's actions—I feel it." It was then Colbie decided to shoot straight. "You see, Mrs. Stanton, when I say I feel something, it's usually true. I enjoy a career as an intuitive private investigator, solving many worldwide cases." A pause. "So, perhaps you'd like to be up front with me . . ."

"Intuitive? You mean you're psychic?"

"Well, yes—and, my ability serves me well." Another pause. "I may as well be blunt, Mrs. Stanton . . ." Addressing Elaine formally was a tactic Colbie used for years, knowing it gave the subliminal impression of authority. "I feel as if you know much more than you're saying . . ."

"Are you saying I'm lying?"

"No—I'm simply saying I don't feel as if you've been forthcoming. If that's the case, you can find yourself in worse circumstances than you're in now . . ."

Elaine stood, her feathers obviously ruffled. "I don't know what you're talking about! But, as I said, I don't have to tell you anything—you're nothing! You're not a cop, so why should I say a word about anything?"

"Please, Elaine, sit down . . ." Time for the soft touch. "Let me help you—everything you said is right. But, I know I can help you if you tell me the truth."

"The truth about what?"

"Walker Newton."

At the mention of his name, Elaine's knees buckled slightly, forcing her to once again take her seat across from Colbie. "I told you . . ."

"I don't believe you, Elaine—I think you knew Walker Newton, and you knew him well. In fact, I feel it's safe to say you two were rather cozy, if you know what I mean . . ."

That's when the veneer cracked.

Elaine's eyes filled with tears as she reached for a tissue in her dress pocket. The same dress she wore when taking care of issues she had with Mr. Newton—although, it probably wasn't the best decision to keep it, take it to a dry cleaner in a nearby town, and wear it whenever she was feeling particularly brash. Concern of discovery simply didn't occur to her—after all, she paid a small fortune for that dress, and it was still perfectly fit to wear after a good cleaning.

She dabbed at her eyes, smearing her makeup in the process, revealing circles a little darker than usual—something not making it past Colbie's investigative eye. "Elaine," she coaxed, "I know what Eric does to you . . ."

"I don't know what you mean . . ."

"Okay—again, I'll be blunt. I know your husband beats the crap out of you, and you take it like a good little wife." She paused, wondering if she went too far. "Is that about it, Elaine?"

Silence.

"I also know—and, there's evidence proving so—that you were in Walker Newton's home. Is that correct?"

Of course, there wasn't really evidence, but Colbie's intuition told her the detective investigating the case would soon find something incriminating—a clue they missed previously.

Again, Elaine gently dabbed her eyes. "I told you—my husband is responsible for that man's murder! Not me!"

Colbie said nothing, knowing the senator's wife could very well be right. Her gut, however, told her differently, convincing her not to abandon her approach. "Then, convince me, Elaine! I can help you!" Another silence, but only for a few seconds. "The cops are going to be at your door, and when they show up?" Colbie waited for an answer, knowing there would be none. "You'll be on your way to jail, Elaine—is that what you want?"

A sniffle. "No . . ."

Suddenly, Colbie stood, taking a seat next to Elaine on the couch. Then, she took her hand, squeezing it gently. "I know what you're going through—but, believe me, lying isn't going to help."

Then, swiftly, Elaine jerked her hand away, stood, then headed for the front door. "Please leave."

Stunned, Colbie remained seated. "Elaine . . ."

"I have nothing to say to you, so please leave."

With grace, Colbie complied, facing the senator's wife as she reached the door. "I wish you luck, Elaine . . ."

Detective Kilgarry silently chastised himself for not recognizing what Hobbs revealed as true—usually, he prided himself on observing the slightest details. But, if what Hobbs were telling him were the truth, it placed Eric Stanton even more in the crosshairs, spousal abuse being the least of his problems. "Continue . . ."

Hobbs paused, taking a drink of water, the few seconds or so allowing him time to further gather his thoughts. "It wasn't until Harry drew his last breath, Detective, did Eric's trafficking operation ramp up. Until then, it was more of an undercurrent, one regarded as sacred by those involved."

"Right after Harry died?"

"Not really—it took a month or so. But, being in my line of business for as long as I have, Detective, there was no doubt Eric Stanton began making up for lost time . . ."

"Explain."

"Well, after infiltrating Eric's operation, it was obvious to me he enjoyed his time at the helm—something that rarely happened when his father was around. He began making numerous trips to Las Vegas, which Harry never did. He was always careful to never arouse suspicion . . ." Hobbs paused for another swig of water. "In fact, Detective, Harry was so livid about it, he took it upon himself to do a little sleuthing of his own."

Kilgarry continued to scribble notes even though the interview was being recorded. "What kind of sleuthing?"

"Well, I don't know much about it because I had to remain on the fringes except when I was acting in the role of Eric Stanton's private investigator. But, I can tell you, for some reason, Harry and Eric thought one of the senators knew what they were up to."

"Name?"

"Jake Powers."

Kilgarry shook his head slightly. "Does he know what they were up to? The organization?"

"I don't know—all I know about Jake Powers is Eric's mentioning there was something about Powers that gave him the creeps. He had me tail Powers in Seattle, so I put Newton on it."

"What did he find out?"

"Nothing—Powers made him on his second day."

"Duly noted. Since you were ostensibly in the employ of Eric Stanton by that time, what other work did he have you do?"

"Keep an eye on his wife."

"Okay—back to Powers. I thought you just said you don't know much about him . . ."

"I don't—like I said, Newton reported he thought Powers was on to him, so I called off surveillance on the second day—then, Constance got involved."

Kilgarry glanced at Detective Marsh, then focused again on Nash Hobbs. "In what way?"

"Well, Detective, much to my surprise, it turned out Constance Parnell has a fetish for electronic devices—and, a degree in Electrical Engineering was a nice plus, too."

Kilgarry smiled, continuing to write. "That explains the wall of gadgets . . ."

"Indeed, it does—I asked her to electronically surveil Jake Powers to see if he were making trouble for Eric."

"And?"

"Nothing. As I figured at the time, Eric was beginning to lose it—money and power became his modus operandi."

"Okay. You mentioned you were also assigned to Elaine Stanton—why?"

Hobbs was quiet, a further indication he felt a twinge of compassion for the senator's wife. "Because he thought she was steppin' out . . ."

"Was she?"

A nod. "Yep—with Walker Newton."

CHAPTER 28

*T*here are always casualties when choosing to work the other side of the street when it comes to the law. Eric Stanton certainly had no compunction about doing whatever was necessary to ascertain the obscenely enormous amount of wealth he required to maintain his lifestyle. Lives didn't matter, young nor old, nor family allegiances when it came to preserving what he worked so hard to achieve.

"Did you hear," Ryan asked as Colbie sat down in his booth in the hotel restaurant.

"Nope—heard what?"

"Elaine Stanton was found dead early this morning."

Stunned, Colbie stared at her partner. "Are you serious?"

He nodded, then turned his laptop toward her so she could see the screen. "Read it for yourself . . ."

Fishing her reading glasses from her messenger bag, she said nothing as she absorbed the brief, online breaking news article. "Holy crap . . ."

"I know—did you have any inkling of it when you talked to her?"

"No . . ." She focused again on Ryan. "Are you saying she committed suicide?"

"I don't know—maybe. Considering what you told me about your conversation with her, maybe she decided she couldn't take it anymore . . ."

"Or, maybe her husband decided he couldn't take her anymore."

Both were quiet, Colbie wondering if her conversation with Elaine Stanton played a part in her death. "I offered to help her . . ."

"With what?"

Another silence. "I told her I knew about her relationship with Walker Newton . . ."

Ryan's eyebrows arched as he turned the laptop toward him. "But, you didn't know that . . ."

"I know—I had a gut feeling, though, and I went with it."

"If they find out she committed suicide, are you saying your conversation with her had something to do with it?"

"Maybe." A pause. "I don't know . . ."

It was a thought Colbie didn't want to carry with her, yet she knew she would until the situation were resolved.

"Like you said, don't forget about Eric—I have a feeling it's entirely possible he offed her if got pissed enough. Don't forget, you told Daniken you thought she had something to do with Walker Newton's murder—you said you heard two gunshots."

"That's right! But, I didn't think for a second they would be from Elaine's killing herself!"

From Colbie's tone, Ryan could tell the stress was beginning to get to her. "You're not thinking, Colbie—you heard two shots. If Elaine killed herself, there wouldn't be two shots . . ."

"Oh, geez! You're right! So—I either heard the shots murdering Walker Newton, or the shots killing Elaine." She hesitated, thinking about the online news article. "Did it say she was shot twice?"

Ryan shook his head. "Nope—there was barely any information. What you read is what we know . . ."

"Damn."

"The question is where do we go from here? As I see it, we're done . . ."

Colbie agreed. "When it comes down to it, we don't have anything to do with Elaine—only Walker Newton and Eric Stanton. All we were hired to do was find out information about the trafficking ring—and, we did that. Now it's up to the authorities . . .'

"This case didn't pan out like any of our others, that's for sure."

"I know—and, it makes me realize I'm making the right decision."

"About getting out of investigative work?"

A nod. "Yes—I don't feel we did our best work here. It was convoluted, and nothing seems to make sense—when I feel like that, I know something's off. I also know it's time for a change . . ."

Ryan stood, grabbing his jacket. "Well, you won't know until you quit if you made the right decision . . ." He headed for the door, stopping to look at her. "I just hope it won't be too late . . ."

CHAPTER 29

By the end of the week, there wasn't a soul in Washington who didn't know about Elaine Stanton's purported suicide. Of course, there were whispers, some in poor taste, others feeling sorry for her husband, offering appropriate condolences until they were behind closed doors.

Either way, it was a story undoubtedly to continue into the following year.

After a debrief with Frank Arlington, there was little doubt Colbie's and Ryan's work in Vegas was worth the effort. If it hadn't been for spotting Eric Stanton in the alley beside People's First Delivery, they may have never made the connection. Even so, the customary satisfaction of solving a case was missing.

"It's odd," Ryan commented as they packed, both ready to head for home. "I never felt as if we were in control of this investigation . . ."

"Neither did I—and, I think it's going to be a long time before everything is sorted out. At least a year before anyone goes to trial . . ."

"If they go to trial. Don't forget, this is Washington we're dealing with—they're not exactly quick to investigate one of their own."

Colbie laughed. "It depends on what side of the aisle you're on, don't you think?"

"Probably!"

Ryan was quiet, not wanting to bring up the obvious. "So—when do you head to Edinburgh?"

Colbie turned to him, recognizing the hurt in his eyes. "In two weeks—I don't start classes for another month, but I want to get settled before I dive in. It's been a long time since I was in school . . ."

"Especially that kind of school . . ."

Colbie leveled a solid glare. "What's that supposed to mean?"

"Nothing—it's just that you studied Psychology, and diving into the paranormal is going to be different. That's all . . ."

As much as she wanted to believe him, Colbie knew his heart was breaking—hers was, too.

Just not in the same way.

CHAPTER 30

*C*old and raw, rain slapped against the tiny window as twilight delivered its message to prepare for another miserable night. As much as Colbie wanted to believe the unpleasant weather was akin to Seattle's, it really wasn't—Edinburgh's winter offered little solace tucked within its folds of wind and stinging drizzle.

It was during such evenings, recurring thoughts of home plagued her, self-doubt pricking every pleasant thought she managed to muster. Although she visited Scotland's capitol city several times prior to her studying at the university, it was always with a sense of comfort because of her Irish heritage—though they were different, Scotland offered a feeling of home. But, that night?

Nothing but a sense of loss and loneliness.

Regret.

No sense thinking about that now, she chastised herself as she sipped a cup of tea while curled up on the small window bench watching the rain. But, reorienting to a new city, new career, and new life wasn't all it was cracked up to be. Missing expectations is something Colbie refused to admit or acknowledge and, if changes needed to happen, she was at least willing to consider them—or, she used to be.

So, there she sat, flirting with the fringes of her shadow world, wanting to enter, but knowing she shouldn't. It was then her cell chirped, its screen illuminating her face just enough to reveal a certain unhappiness. "Ryan?"

"Yep! It's me!"

It had been too long since they chatted, their parting after returning to Seattle from D.C. less than pleasant. If she were to be honest, her heart raced just a touch at the sound of his voice. "How are you? Where are you?"

A familiar laugh. "I'm fine, and I'm in Seattle."

Colbie would've been lying if she said she weren't a little disappointed. "So, why the call? What's up?"

"I thought you might be interested in the latest developments with the Stanton case . . ." A pause. "But, if you don't want to know what's going on, I completely understand." It was bait he knew would work. The truth was he was thinking of Colbie, and he just wanted to hear her voice.

"You're such a bonehead! Of course, I want to know what's happening!"

"I knew you would!"

Colbie listened as he opened a bottle of water and took a drink before launching into the latest. "So," he finally continued, "it turns out it was just as you thought—Eric Stanton was just arrested for the murder of Costin Dalca."

"Only now? Holy cow! What on earth took them so long? It seemed pretty cut and dried when we left . . ."

"It was, but I suspect political backlash was slow to react until there was formidable proof. Until then, it was pretty much swept under the rug . . ."

"Aided by the media, no doubt . . ." Colbie hesitated, thinking about how much she missed while living in a different country. Then again, she didn't exactly make an effort to keep on top of things—her life was different, and she needed to embrace all changes, good or bad.

"Of course—the biased cogs always keep grinding." A pause. "But, that's not all . . ."

Colbie smiled, once again enjoying Ryan's inimitable way of making her feel good. "Go on . . ."

"Seems your hunch was right—Stanton was also arrested for Elaine's murder."

"What?" Quickly, Colbie cycled through events leading her to suspect Eric. "I knew it!"

Ryan chuckled, delighted he could deliver great news. "Yes, you did—although, to be fair, neither one of us were really sure."

"I know. Well, it's going to be a long time before the trial—what happened regarding People's First?"

"Shut down. Mihai Bucur is cooperating from what I understand, although information in spotty. I check the Vegas online news every now and then, but there hasn't been a lot. The one thing is, though, Jessica hasn't been mentioned as being a suspect in anything, so that's good."

"Excellent! I don't think she had any idea of anything. She seemed more interested in her boyfriend . . ."

Again, Ryan chuckled. "Ahh—to be young again!"

"I know what you mean!" Then, a thoughtful question. "What about the girls?"

"From what I gather, they're trying to figure out where they were placed and with whom. Of course, that's going to be next to impossible—but, at least there won't be any more from Stanton's organization."

"And, what about that? Has there been anything about who was involved?"

"Some—Derrick Dickson finally told his story on one of the news shows, then announced he wouldn't be seeking reelection. Said he's had enough . . ."

"I don't blame him. No charges against him?"

"Nope—and, I don't think there should be. After what he and his family endured, he deserves a pass for whatever offense prosecutors in Stanton's case can drum up."

"Agreed."

"What about Hobbs and Constance?"

Ryan fiddled around with something, asked Colbie to hang on, then returned with a beer. "Sorry—I'm out of water, and I think we should celebrate!" Then, the familiar sound of a beer-can whoosh. "So, to continue—I found this out only a couple of days ago. It turns out Hobbs and Parnell were the good guys . . ."

"Seriously?"

"Yep—both are flapping their jaws about everything, including how they infiltrated Eric Stanton's trafficking ring to find out everything they could. Then, they were going to go to the cops . . ."

"I don't know, Ryan. It's a good story, but . . ."

"Well, apparently it must be true, but both of us know they probably wouldn't be talking without promise of immunity."

"True."

"What grabbed me was Constance Parnell—who knew she held a Masters of Electrical Engineering? She was the one responsible for surveilling your buddy, Jake . . ."

A dig?

Maybe a little one.

Colbie said nothing as realization struck. "You know— we really were on the periphery of this whole thing. Listening to what you're saying, we suspected, but never had solid proof of anything. All of that came by the work of detectives, and all the people who were involved after we left." A pause. "We really did nothing . . ."

"I don't think that's true . . ."

"I do—and, it's proof it was time for me to leave it behind."

"Do you regret it?"

"Sometimes . . ."

"What about what you're doing now? Is it everything you thought it would be?"

"Sometimes."

So, there they sat on opposite sides of the world, Colbie listening to winter's fury, wondering if she did the right thing, Ryan feeling the loss of the only woman in his life he ever truly loved.

Yet, neither said a word.

As her cell screen faded to black, Colbie closed her eyes, missing Ryan and the life she knew. Regrets? More than one. But, there was no sense attempting to turn back time—a realization causing more than a little angst. It was a drag, too—what Colbie thought was the perfect solution to her problems turned out to be symptomatic of shadow work needing to be done.

It was then Colbie heard it—a faint whisper.

Slowly, she opened her eyes, her friend standing in front of her. "Daria . . ."

A ghostly smile. "You have nothing to feel badly about," Daria whispered. "You're following the path you were meant to take—and, I will always be here to guide you." Another smile. "Accept your future, Colbie." Daria paused as she began to fade.

"And, life will be yours . . ."

THE COLBIE COLLEEN
MYSTERY SUSPENSE SERIES!

The Accidental Audience

Chasing Rhinos

Apology Accepted

Whiskey Snow

Chill of Deception

At the Intersection of Blood & Money

The Scent of Unfinished Business

Agenda

COMING IN SPRING, 2021!

Where Truth Goes to Die
a Decklin Kilgarry Suspense Mystery, Book 1

PROFESSIONAL ACKNOWLEDGMENTS

CHRYSALIS PUBLISHING AUTHOR SERVICES

L.A. O'Neil, Editor

www.chrysalis-pub@gmail.com

chrysalispub@gmail.com

Manufactured by Amazon.ca
Bolton, ON

20686327R00164